D1636798

Law and Order

by

CLAUDE OLLIER

Translated from the French by
URSULE MOLINARO

Red Dust • New York

Translated by Ursule Molinaro
with thanks to Venable Herndon

Originally published in France as
Le Maintien de l'Ordre
    ©1961 Librarie Gallimard
    This translation:
    ©1971 Red Dust Inc.
Library of Congress Catalogue Card
                number 76-133248
Standard Book Number
                87376- 015-8

Printed by: Universal Lithographers Inc.
Bound by: L. H. Jenkins, Inc.

LAW AND ORDER

A large uniform screen stretches, smooth, from one end of the horizon to the other. On it sparkles a thin pale dust; a greyish moisture veils the vibrating air, the eddying water. All the way up, big clouds come floating in from the open sea, pile up, break up, slowly drift off to the north; below, long waves unfurl, explode at the crests, stretch over the flat rocks along the shore. In between, in the intermediary zone, the transition is imperceptible: sky and ocean fuse in a translucid, lead-colored stuff. Nothing separates them, no dividing line: everywhere the same filtered light, with its cutting, blinding glare.

Further down, etched on a smaller plate, countless straight lines form a system of unequal rectangles, joined perpendicularly like the panels of a mould, some rising straight up --the large new housefronts along the shore, fences, embankments of red clay on the periphery of the old city--, most of them stacked horizontally, in no apparent order --sheds, warehouse roofs, terraced native houses, criss-crossed by white-washed pigmy walls. Wash dries on the terraces: hundreds of pieces of cloth, flapping in the wind.

Somewhat closer, the green square of Wilson Park. Two wide diagonal paths cross a circle dominated by a statue. Around the circle, dry lawn, bordered by monkey-puzzles and palms, their drab bluish foliage at the moment completely stilled. On the edge of the park two parallel rows of eucalyptus trees, their lower branches hardly move, only the tops sway.

Still closer, alongside the trees, the grounds of the *Bocce* club, squeezed between park and avenue: on the left roofed structures --bar, locker rooms, restaurant-- on the right the alleys --eight rectangles of ochre-colored earth, separated by low wooden dividers. It is too early for the players. A young barefoot boy is fingering a nozzle trailing a long black rubber hose behind it. He brandishes the nozzle obliquely skyward: the water rises in a shimmering mirror and comes down as rain.

Very close, though invisible, a hoarse-horned bus passes on the avenue far below. The motor noise and the shivering street reverberate through the whole building, from the stoop with its wrought-iron railings all the way up to the top floor windows.

The wide open windows vibrate, the thin walls of the room vibrate, the door of the room vibrates and outside, two steps out into the hall, the door of the elevator cage vibrates, longer, duller, since it's heavier. Although perhaps it would vibrate anyway, without the rumbling of the bus...Perhaps it is still vibrating from the brusque slamming, scarcely a couple of seconds ago, that brutal hasty slamming, an instant or so before the bursting into the room, and the more precise, almost soothing slamming of the door of the room --a fragile bulwark, a first support to lean against, facing the wide open window, a first halt, a pause, the few seconds needed to catch one's breath.

The elevator door is still vibrating: as though the iron knob were still shivering inside a hand.

The bus drives off: the trembling decreases. Several cars pass in its wake, their only traces the clear, high-pitched sound of their motors punctuated by two extremely brief tootings of a horn. After that, no more cars on the avenue...The window panes have stopped vibrating, and the walls of the room, and the door. All seems calm, beyond the door as well. The elevator has not budged: it must still be at the same floor where it stopped a minute ago. And nobody has had the time to walk up seven flights.

Besides, there is no sign of anybody climbing the stairs, at least not as far as the upper floors. Not a sound filters through the wooden panel: no rhythm of footfalls, no furtive scraping on the imitation marble steps, no sound of shoes bumping into banister spindles...Everything is quiet. If anybody is climbing the stairs, he must be pretty far down.

Better make sure, though, just in case, since there's still time...Still time to open the door again and look out onto the landing.

The knob clicks, the tongue slides out of the slot, slowly the door swings on its hinges: through the opening appear the top steps of the stairs, then the banister spindles and, a little further to the left, behind the banister, the iron-grilled shaft that surges out of the depths of the building, shoots still a few yards higher, to the roof which it seems to pierce with its metal stems.

The elevator is still sitting in the same place, empty, motionless, inside the grillwork: it plugs up the stairwell, concealing the spirals of the lower floors. To see what goes on below, one must walk down some ten steps --but first push out the bolt to make sure the wind won't slam the door shut with a lot of noise--, then peep under the elevator, through the grillwork, a system of black-painted criss-crossing distorted lozenges. At that point the field of vision widens considerably. It includes the entire sixth-floor landing, the first and last thirds of the flight between the sixth and fifth floors, most of the fifth-floor landing, two further although much more limited sections of the fifth-to-fourth flight, and approximately half of the fourth-floor landing...Further down the grillwork hides almost all other parts of the staircase that should theoretically be visible: the third-floor landing is reduced to a narrow longitudinal strip outside the elevator door, the second-floor landing is completely invisible as is, obviously, that of the first floor and, of course, the ground floor.

Nothing stirs. Not a sound climbs the stairs. But this impression of emptiness cannot be trusted: someone might easily sneak up as far as the third floor without being seen, and even further, rapidly ducking into one of the unobservable areas between floors, and wait there, concealed in frozen silence, as long as anyone might be watching.

Going down to the sixth-floor landing wouldn't do much good: the enemy would promptly resort to a parallel stratagem. The same situation would repeat itself halfway between the sixth and fifth floors, then on the fifth-floor landing, and so forth, from floor to floor, all the way down. Into the foyer, and out onto the stoop; from there into the avenue. And once in the avenue, once outside...Once outside, the maneuver would start all over again, and in that case what would be the use of having gone up in the first place?

Unless they suddenly decide to hurry things, to get it over with right here and now, anywhere the opportunity presents itself, right here, for instance, on the sixth-floor landing, further down even, in spite of the other tenants who would inevitably hear shots, or simply scuffling noises. No, no; these are unnecessary fears: the risk is much too great, in the staircase, especially on the lower floors, where most of the tenants stay shut up in their apartments throughout the day.

The cleverest tactic would probably be to stand in the stairs and keep watch --to close the door to the room, to send the elevator back down to unblock the field of vision, and alternate look-out stations between the seventh-floor landing and right here, halfway between the two floors, to alternate regularly between the two floors in order to frustrate any attempted approach.

But how long a wait would it be? Nothing suggests the immediacy of the event, or its probability even. Besides, the interference of a third person might blur the traces at any moment, create misunderstandings, unpleasantly ambiguous situations and harmful delays. All things carefully considered, it is preferable to go back to the room and lock oneself in, and to sneak out on the landing from time to time, to see if the situation is still the same.

Exactly halfway between the two floors, a sliding window has been cut into the outside wall of the house; it faces east, toward the business district of the European section. It is closed as usual, its cord torn off a few inches below the latch which is out of reach.

If one climbs back up five or six steps, one can see on the other side of the glass, far below, a fenced-in, deeply furrowed vacant lot. It looks abandoned: the walls of the excavation have collapsed in spots; weeds and brambles grow on the mounds of earth. Further away, the eye stumbles upon the blind wall of a large building...The window pane is filthy, bygone showers have streaked it with greyish vertical lines that form a second coarser, more irregular veil, speckled with shiny grains --impurities in the glass or splashes from bad weather-- between the eye and sun-soaked mist that tones down the glare of the stone.

At closer inspection, the stairway is almost as filthy, but the layer of dust --which is particularly thick along the wall and close to the banister-- is practically the same color as the imitation marble.

On the seventh-floor landing the dust is more apparent, on the grey-pink composition material imitating sandstone as well as on its mosaic border: five parallel rows of small squares, alternately black and yellow. Imitation sandstone and mosaic border have not been swept since the week before: an inch of string, matches, a crumpled-up newspaper band lie in front of the elevator.

The door to the first apartment on the left is closed. The tenant is a bank clerk or an insurance agent, and he is away at work; he doesn't come home before seven o'clock. The draft has gradually closed the second door facing the stairs, but the tongue of the lock sticks out and keeps it from slamming.

The two apartments at the other end of the landing are empty: the tenants, two childless couples, have been away on vacation since the first of the month. A visiting card with gothic lettering (Mr. & Mrs. Renard), slipped into a copper frame, occupies the center of the last door.

Beside that door on the right, a metal ladder lies on its side, partly against the wall and partly against the last stretch of banister that runs beyond the elevator, and marks the end of the stairs. A trap door in the ceiling leads to the terrace; it is kept padlocked.

A large figure 7 sprawls on the wall facing the elevator, at equal distance between the two clusters of doors. Its slanting bar is at least two inches wide and drawn by a great many angry, chaotic pencil strokes, as though the hand had become impatient at one point, and in a hurry to finish...

A brief, surprisingly clear tinkling echoes up the stairwell, followed by a spray of many clicks, very much like a handful of marbles or dimes thrown violently on a tile floor: they scatter; bounce from step to step...Then a grunt, a curse, another tinkling and after a long silence, the sound of slow regular steps, punctuated by throat-clearing --a negligently put-on slipper slurring on the steps. The sound mounts, comes closer...After a pause of several seconds, the crossing of the landing probably, the pounding starts up again, with more precision --one-two-- louder now --six-seven-eight-- always at the same moderate, placid cadence. At seventeen, there is an interruption, the ringing starts again, more sharply, a tinkling of small bells, the sound of keys manipulated by clumsy fingers. Soon there is a slam, instantaneous, quickly suffocated, and then another slam, much louder, violent, final, and its repercussions for a long time, from bottom to top, from top to bottom, weaving back and forth with decreasing intensity, from bottom to top, from top to bottom, all the way up and down the stairwell.

The steel banister railing quivers slightly under one's fingers.

The elevator is still sitting in the same spot: it didn't seem worth calling it down to go to the second floor; it has stayed there, immobile, empty, stopped slightly below the level of the landing.

All is quiet once more. Nothing moves on the stairs. Only the muffled echo of noises from the avenue, still filtering in through the half-open door, troubles the silence.

Closer to the door the noise gains precision, grows louder, and the instant the door swings on its hinges, rapidly disclosing the left half of the room (night table, bed, bookcase, armchair), motor noises fill the air again and a puff of heat escapes and disturbs for a few seconds the closed-in, much cooler air of the hall.

The door swings open, all at once disclosing the other half of the room (table, chair, wardrobe, bathroom door). A red-patterned wool rug hides the major part of the imitation sandstone floor and stretches with slight undulations all the way up to the foot of the window.

The door knob clicks. The tongue of the lock is drawn back before it penetrates the slot, in two movements.

The motor noise of the cars that pass on the avenue is punctuated by more or less loud, more or less sustained horn blasts, sometimes extremely brief, sometimes repeated in rapid succession, with an insistence betraying exasperation. A bus drives by, recognizable by its loud horn and the quaking it communicates to the entire house front at the exact moment it passes the stoop. The door of the room --though locked-- vibrates, as does the elevator door outside two steps out onto the landing. The walls of the room vibrate, and the wide-open windows.

The avenue, its trees and sidewalks, some twenty-five to thirty yards down are not visible from the door of the room, neither is the wall around the *Bocce* club, nor the lawn where children are allowed to play. But nobody is there yet; the grounds are deserted. Nor has the boy finished sprinkling them; he is slowly moving the nozzle at the right height: the water falls like rain on the tamped ochre-colored earth.

Further up, the eucalyptus trees move phlegmatic fronds. The paths through Wilson Park are also practically deserted. They become animated only later in the afternoon, when the offices let out.

On the roofs of the old city, on the other side of the park, countless pieces of cloth are flapping in the wind, which makes the flat surfaces and linear outlines of the buildings look as though they were continuously, almost imperceptibly shivering.

Above the checkerboard maze of the terraces, the humidity from the ocean has woven a vast translucid veil through which a pale, silver-grey dust sparkles: sky and ocean blend, everywhere the same sharp blinding light comes filtering through.

The distance from door to window is slightly less than twelve feet, staked out by the geometric patterns of the rug: advancing toward the window rapidly widens one's field of vision.

Already with the first step the horizon expands noticeably. All at once several new details stand out in the landscape: a group of tall houses on the right; on the left the façade and towers of the cathedral; at the top, a long rectangle of clouds; all the way down, a strip of lawn.

With the second step: the lighthouse at the tip of the elbowed jetty; the nave of the cathedral; a new fringe of clouds; a larger surface of lawn jump into view.

With the third: a row of cranes, an ocean liner maneuvering in the harbor; way behind the cathedral, in the southern suburb, the villas and pines of the residential sections; a broad stretch of sky bordering the zenith; the wall around the *Bocce* club.

And finally: the factories in the northern industrial suburbs; the line of hills that mark the southern limits of the city; the darker vault of the sky directly overhead; the acacias along the other sidewalk across the avenue and, closer by, two thirds of the asphalt paving.

For a view of the entire street and the sidewalk outside the building, one only needs to lean out slightly, with both hands on the window sill...The ball-round tops of the acacias conceal part of the sidewalk and of the street. Along the curb, cars are parked practically bumper to bumper; some are hidden under the leaves, but most of them are completely visible.

The big black car is there, parked in front of the building, slightly to the left of the entrance. Perez is sitting behind the wheel; Marietti, rag in hand, is polishing the radiator grill. Perez is talking, his fingers are drumming on the gear shift. Marietti answers something, gestures, points to something on the hood. Perez shrugs and braces his back against the seat.

Marietti stops rubbing and stands motionless for a second, torso bent slightly forward, both hands on the radiator grill. Then he straightens up, turns toward the building and slowly raises his head toward the upper floors...

On the opposite sidewalk the small yellowish acacia leaves barely move --the avenue is never very windy-- nor do the flaming-iris leaves that border the lawn on the other side of the brick wall. The young club employee has finished watering the grounds. He goes into the shed next to the locker rooms, comes out again a few seconds later, dragging a rotating nozzle which he sets up near the wall, on the part of the lawn that is farthest away from the buildings. Then he goes back to screw the end of the long black rubber hose onto the spigot.

Farther away, on the street that leads from rue Lamarck to the gate of the club, the first players arrive at a leisurely pace.

The clock over the locker room says five fifteen.

Yesterday is repeating itself, and the day before yesterday, with a few slight variations: a few minutes apart the same gestures, the same looks; a few yards farther or closer the same steps, the same retreats, the same maneuvers. In a little while Marietti will slip into the front seat; a moment later Perez will climb out, walk back and forth under the trees, cross the avenue, sit down on the bench, comfortably, with legs crossed and arms stretched out at shoulder level placidly resting on the wooden back...About six Marietti takes the wheel, starts the motor, drives as far as the square in front of the park gates, turns, comes back and parks the car along the curb on the other side of the avenue, close to Perez' bench. At this point Peres' nose is turned skyward, he is smoking a cigarette. Soon Marietti gets out and sits down beside him. Then both get up, as they did yesterday, cross the avenue, immobilized midway by the stream of traffic. They head toward the building, step up on the sidewalk, disappear under the trees, reappear, walk toward the entrance, disappear again...The sidewalk is deserted. The footsteps of the two men echo on the stoop, in the hall, outside the janitor's door, finally on the bottom stairs. The elevator cage begins to vibrate; its long metal stems vibrate all the way up to the seventh floor; the door of the room vibrates, the walls vibrate, the windows, the entire house front is vibrating, from the wrought-iron entrance door all the way up to the seventh-floor windows...But it was only a trick. They stayed down in the hall for a couple of minutes, then reappeared on the sidewalk, walked gingerly back to the car, climbed in, one in the front, the other in the back, both comfortably stretched out. Perez bought the evening paper from a boy who ran past, read it for about half an hour, then handed it to Marietti who read it too...At eight they drove off, like yesterday. It was beginning to get dark. Most of the players had left. The few who had stayed later soon went into the club restaurant. After dinner other players --or the same-- came back, large lamps were turned on in the trees, the games continued until late into the night.

The window had remained open, the blind pulled up. The lighthouse illuminated the room. At regular pedantic intervals the sheaf of light that swept the coast burst into the room, hastily projected the shadow of the window onto the walls --two horizontal bars, the latch, the outlines of the curtains-- the shadow of the candlestick on the table, of the perfume burner on the corner of the shelf, and fled, leaving the image of the objects that had been briefly caught in a funnel of brightness imprinted on the brain.

The voices of evening strollers rose up from the avenue, the purring of cars, the trumpeting of a bus; and from the other side the clicking of balls, and players shouting; and from the park the monotonous chafing of the crickets; from farther away the notes of flutes and violins in the alleys of the old section; and from still farther away the sound of the surf.

Far away, suddenly very close, far away again, very near, the sound of the surf filled the room, cradled the sleeplessness. About two a.m. fog invaded the coast, rapidly shrouded the land from the shore to the center of the city. The sound of the surf grew almost inaudible. At the far-out tip the fog horn began to moo its grave drawn-out laments, as though they were coming from an island or from the bottom of the sea.

Still later, the muffled signals, punctuated by uneven notes,

The lighthouse stands on the tip of the jetty, beyond the ship basins and rows of mobile cranes, standing only a little taller than the tallest crane. The ocean liner which was pulling away from the pier a little while ago and ploughing through the harbor is now about to pass the jetty. Its white hull hardly heaves; it passes at right angles to the grey stone embankment and looks as though it were going to ram smack into the last few yards of rock. The gap between bow and lighthouse is narrowing slowly, imperceptibly, the different stages of the movement escape the eye, suddenly the stern attacks the lighthouse, as if to slice it in half at the middle, a joining of vertical lines, a fusion, a stacking of levels...The first funnel of the ship is already sliding past the jetty.

Further out from the shore, above (or still below) the line of the horizon, the eye straining toward the ocean sees only a grey uniform dust shimmer above the warehouses, sheds and stacked-up terraces: the roofs of the modern apartment houses recently built along the water front to uncrowd the old Jewish quarter.

Closer, on the periphery of the park, the dull, dusty leaves of the eucalyptus trees, of undecided color, a mixture of light green, pale yellow and grey. The palms in the center reflect purple tints. The monkey-puzzles around the central circle break this uniformity with their short, strictly horizontal branches at different heights, neat and precise as though punched out of zinc plate by a machine. Birds --gulls?-- are circling around the statue whose right arm is pointing inland as though giving the signal for an invasion. Its grey-white stone helmet, with the visor raised skyward, stands out against the yellow lawn.

The sculptured arm, the hand with its chiseled-out finger, point east, to the lands that are to be conquered: the sad, sun-singed fields, the rocky hills, the forests of spiny bushes, and still farther away, towering mountain chains, deserted summits where lumps of snow lie all through the summer, protected from the sun in crevices of slate.

But the sweeping martial gesture is halted by a ridiculous obstacle immediately after the first curtain of trees: a couple of wooden structures, a restaurant, a bar and, farther to the right, the play grounds: eight rectangles of ochre-colored earth, separated by low wooden dividers.

The boy is squatting on his heels, on the pebble walk outside the locker rooms, through the tall poinsettia stems he examines the smooth lawn, a smooth green it stretches for some twenty yards up to another row of bushes along the brick wall. Behind the wall, behind the smooth stretch of green, he sees the house front, seven cement floors rising on the opposite side of the avenue, without balconies, without ledges, with regularly spaced long bay windows that overlook the ocean.

A foot away, behind the iron wickets of the lawn, the elbow-shaped water pipe sticks out of the ground like a periscope; the hose is attached to it. If he reaches out, he can touch the spigot.

The first players who, a little while ago, came strolling up to the club entrance have disappeared into the bar, or perhaps into the locker rooms --but they were in shirt sleeves when they arrived, they wouldn't be long in the locker rooms--. In a little while they'll re-emerge from either place and walk straight over to the first alley. Another group of four men is already turning the corner of rue Lamarck, coming up the road.

By now the large hand of the clock has joined and passed the small hand: it is sliding toward the half hour. The boy is still squatting on his heels, he bends slightly forward, reaches --the clock hand moves, quivers --the boy reaches for the spigot --the clock hand settles into vertical position-- the boy has his hand on the spigot.

The spigot turns. Immediately the hose begins to writhe, a loop at the edge of the lawn unloops, halfway down there is a leak, very straight a thin jet of water blurts out, a few seconds before the fan-shaped twin-spray unfolds at the extremities of the nozzle. The copper nozzle is solidly mounted, horizontal on its tripod; slowly it starts to spin. The water shoots out, arcs, falls as rain.

Drops fall on the flaming-iris spears, they bend, stand up, bend again; probably they also fall on the brick wall of the enclosure, on the tiles that top the wall, perhaps some even fall behind the wall, on the sidewalk of the avenue, when a gust of wind shifts the nozzle to a certain angle.

But acacia leaves mask that piece of the sidewalk: its small yellow bevel-edged stones disappear under a chaos of branches and pale green leaves. Closer to the avenue they blend into an uninterrupted strip, about a yard wide, all the way up to the granite curb. The wooden bench stands between two trees, exactly opposite the window; like all the other benches along the avenue it is empty; normally nobody sits there. The cars pass at a steady speed, the pedestrians walk close to the walls, no one comes here to stroll, no one stops --further down: yes, on the square just before the park, or farther up, by the sidewalk cafes. But never here; here people only pass, because they have to pass this way.

The west side of the avenue is deserted: the red light at the park square has stopped the cars. Except for a child on a man's bicycle zig-zagging close to the curb, as though he'd been forgotten; he can't sit on the saddle, his legs are too short, they churn as best they can, spasmodically, holding a swaying balance on the pedals.

One only has to lean out a little, both hands on the window sill, to span half the avenue in a glance; the trees, the sidewalk in front of the building.

Cars are coming by on this side of the avenue, Indian file toward the harbor. As expected, the big black Buick has not moved. Marietti has finished polishing the hood. Now he is shining up the chrome headlight rims and the bumper. As on the preceding days he is wearing a red and black checkered shirt with short sleeves, sunglasses and grey linen trousers. He has left his dark blue jacket inside the car. Seen from the window, his silhouette seven floors below is reduced to the black ball of his cream-oiled hair, to broad shoulders and hairy arms moving about the front of the car, to two hands clutching a rag running back and forth, up and down the bumper.

Perez is stretched out across the front seat.

Now several cars arrive from the harbor, trailed by a yellow bus, all its metal panels loose, clanking and rattling. In the opposite direction the flow has been stopped, probably by the red light on Roosevelt Square a little farther down to the left, three hundred yards away.

Marietti stops polishing. He stands up straight, fists on hips he is inspecting his work. He looks right, looks left, stares after some people passing on the sidewalk, steps up on the curb, walks up to the car door, through the open window he slips the rag into the glove compartment on the right.

Then, without turning around, without attempting to look up even, he opens the door, lowers his head and slides into the seat. The door slams.

Perez has slightly rectified his position to make room for his colleague. His knees are pulled up under the wheel. The fingers of his right hand are drumming on the gear shift, but only for a second, already the left door is opening, his long body extricates itself from the car, first the half-bald head, then the white cotton sweater, finally the legs, with red socks showing under the khaki trouser cuffs. The door slams.

Slowly Perez crosses the avenue, stops midway to let the cars go by, they are now passing in both directions, then he walks briskly forward, steps up on the curb, sits down on the bench, legs crossed, arms stretched out at shoulder level, resting on the wooden back.

Marietti sits alone in the big black Buick, it is an old model, but unmistakable because it has no windshield. He examines himself in the rear-view mirror, takes a comb from his shirt pocket and begins to comb his hair with sharp turns of the wrist.

Perez sits comfortably on the bench on the other side of the avenue, just opposite the building; slowly he lifts his head toward the top floors...

Below, the old section of the city looks shrunken to a short slope of steps built along a few hundred yards of shore line, like a stadium with its back to the ocean. Actually the high terraces are quite close to Spanish Square and the European quarters. Behind them lies most of the old city which cannot be seen from here, and still farther away, to the north-west, is the point with the old lighthouse which is no longer in use.

Seen from here the terraced outlines continue clearly all the way west and to the south as far as Spanish Square. But the square itself is hidden by modern buildings around Wilson Park, farther to the right the embankments of Marine Boulevard appear at only one point, halfway between the square and the harbor, exactly in the direction of the Office: if the flag pole were a couple of yards higher, one could see the flag flapping above the roofs.

It took me a long time, today, to get out of the Office. The people turned to leave, pretended to be leaving, but changed their minds before they got out into the street, came back, stood in line again, waited in the courtyard. It was past four o'clock. The corridor was still crowded: there was no end to the various whisperings, consultations, slurring of slippers and sandals on the tiles; the sound of it kept coming through the closed door.

The shutters had been closed since early morning, as usual, for fear of the heat, but the glare is so powerful that the little that does filter in, is always enough to light the room adequately --desk, papers, telephone, visitors' chairs, steel filing cabinet, wooden coat locker, the map of the old city tacked to the wall behind the armchair.

Saïd appeared at once, as usual, at the first brief tinkle of the bell, pushing the door closed behind him, flattening himself against it, his hands clasped around the knob behind his back. He listened without saying a word, without even a nod, then spun on his heels, opening the door just enough to slide through without brushing against it, disappearing soundlessly.

His rusty voice echoed through the corridor where the noise swelled for a few minutes, climaxing in a strident female protest; then Saïd got the upper hand again, invoked Allah, shooed everybody out and planted himself outside the entrance, on the top step, hand on hip, impervious.

-Tomorrow! Nine o'clock!

Saïd pivots, glides, disappears. Does his job smoothly, without brutality...

The people cross the courtyard in small groups, dragging their feet, slowly they pass through the gate, scatter into rue Fayard. The courtyard is empty...

It must be pratically empty at this hour. Bits of straw, olive pits, scraps of paper litter the ground, oil stains dot the cement which the slats of the shutters cut up into narrow parallel rectangles --straight rectangles of white clarity, of kept-out heat, ready to expand into blinding sheets, into puffs of stifling air. If one so much as opens the door, without even stepping into the corridor: the suffocating wave breaks over the threshold of the office, strikes the forehead, the eyes; blood mounts to the head, the lids blink, the throat tightens, the legs feel like lead, move sluggishly.

Motionless, hand on hip, Saïd was standing guard on the stoop outside the entrance. Promptly he drew aside, walked down the steps, headed across the courtyard toward the garage.

At this hour of the day the courtyard lies in full sunlight, except for a shoreline of shade to the west, at the foot of the mosque wall, where it is even hotter than inside the office. The garage is at the north end. To the east, facing the mosque, is the chief's office.

The interpreter came running, suddenly standing at the garage door, panting, saying:

-The chief wants to see you right away. Someone on the phone.

He was sitting at his desk, leaning forward as usual, his elbows solidly anchored on the desk blotter, its four triangular corners stuffed with small slips of paper scribbled full of annotations. His glasses had been pushed up on the damp, sweatglistening forehead, his right hand was pressed flat over the mouthpiece.

First he excused himself, as usual (I'm terribly sorry, you

had asked to leave early, I'm holding you up...). He articulates his excuses, his free hand scratches his nose, his eyebrows rise, his forehead creases (I have Inspector Lacoste on the phone...). He frees his right hand, pulls his handkerchief out of a pocket, pushes his glasses down, wipes his forehead (Yes, Inspector, yes, hang on, I've sent for him, I...), pushes his glasses back up, again his hand is flattened over the mouthpiece (He's coming to see me at eleven tomorrow to put an end to...), looks up, immediately looks elsewhere, as usual, (Yes, that business from last Saturday, of course. I wanted to know if you'd be in...Fine...You understand...), staring at his appointment book now, at the desk blotter, the ink pot, the files that are stacked on his desk to the right (...in everybody's interest, no matter what your objections...to settle the matter as quickly as possible); his free hand is playing with a piece of paper (But I'd like us to agree beforehand), crumples up the paper, throws it into the basket at the left of the desk (Yes, I know, I appreciate your reservations, believe me...), again his eyes look up, very briefly, look down at once (...really don't see what you'd gain from a showdown), his right hand goes back to the handkerchief, rapidly wipes the sweaty forehead, goes back into the pocket (...open the whole thing up again, by a spectacular, but somewhat impulsive decision), his hand is back over the mouthpiece (Nobody would be any better off for it, on either side), pulls away almost immediately, his shoulders straighten (Well, you still have until tomorrow to think it over), his arm stretches across the desk (Right, I'll drop over before eleven). A nod. A fleeting smile (See you tomorrow). The head turns back to the phone. (Hello? Inspector? Hello? Yes, I...), his back rounds forward, his chest bends over the desk, as usual, elbows solidly anchored on the blotter.

The interpreter was pacing in the corridor. A group of women were talking softly. Other women stood waiting in the courtyard in the blazing sun, holding folders, papers tied in a kerchief.

Saïd was still standing in front of the garage door, alert, ready to go through the usual routine (open the wooden doors all the way, walk into the garage, open the front door of the little Fiat, close it, take up a position in the middle of the court-yard, direct the backing out, run to the street, look left, look right, give the clear signal, wave his arm, salute).

The image of Saïd standing in front of the entrance in rue Fayard, under the droopy flag, shrinks in the rear-view mirror, grows tiny, suddenly it has disappeared: one can only turn right, at the end of rue Fayard, there is no other direction --all the streets are one-way in the old Arab section--, then left, twenty yards ahead (rue Zaïda, rue du Port), left again (ten yards: rue des Moines), right (fifty yards of curve: rue El-Hadid), blowing one's horn at each intersection to avoid brutal collisions, although there's never much traffic in this quarter in the late afternoon. Another right turn, and the last, very narrow street (rue des Savetiers) leads through the red rag-stone archway out into Marine Boulevard, at the border of the modern city. There is no other way to drive out of the old city from the Office, unless one backs down certain streets or disobeys the one-way signs.

Marine Boulevard slopes softly down to the port. Before coming to a dead end against the high ramparts of the city wall, it cuts perpendicularly across the ocean drive which comes from the right of the industrial sections and runs left all the way around the old city, toward the western beaches, the swimming pools, the prosperous Aïn Zurka suburb, and still farther, into the dunes and the south coast shore.

It was twenty to five on the big clock in front of the harbor gate. A moving van towing a trailer was slowly creeping along the road that wound its way between iron fences and embank-ments. It blocked the vision and made passing impossible. The little car was bouncing on the pavement; its front bumper shaking and rattling, still twisted and loose from the other day. Many cars passed in the opposite direction. A wine truck appeared in the oval rear-view mirror: the barrels were tied with thick rope and stood very tall, piled in pyramids of five, behind the driver's cab. The other truck, in front, was still advancing at a walking pace, hardly increasing its speed at the end of a curve, at the jetty it was stopped by a dump truck, stopped again, a few yards farther, behind a broken-down cart, at the point where the road crosses the driveway of the old lighthouse. It meant waiting for the cobblestones to end, for the wide straight drive along the shore to begin, before trying to pass.

At last, the Moorish tower appeared on the right, and soon after, on the left, the network of outer boulevards. The road was clear. A prudent reflex, before trying to pass, raised the eyes toward the rear-view mirror: which was no longer reflecting the wine truck: a large black car had taken its place, the old windshieldless Buick was rolling some ten yards behind the little Fiat, exactly in line with it, its mirror image bouncing at every bump in the asphalt. Perez was driving, his right hand on the wheel, the left stuck out through the open window drumming on the chrome searchlight mounted on the windshield stanchion. Marietti was leaning against the seat, both arms stretched across the back, his feet on the dashboard; his black glasses glistening in the gap between the soles of his shoes.

The truck was moving a little faster. It was nearing the new buildings with their many-colored façades; it was conscientiously holding to the right of the road, leaving a free strip of some ten yards on the left.

The little Fiat pulled out of its lane and moved up beside the moving van when the bigger car shot up alongside, coming very close very fast, veering sharply quickly in front of it, crowding it toward the truck.

The rear wheels skidded as the brakes were jammed on, the hood swerved to the right, brushing against the thick tires of the truck. The van passed a few inches from the fender, slowly, ponderously, its chassis on a level with the door handles.

The motor had stalled. The car stood immobilized in the middle of the road, unhurt, turned at an angle toward the ocean, toward the tamarisk hedge planted along the promenade, on the high ridge above the rocks.

The wine truck passed next. The driver leaned out of his cab, screaming curses. Other cars followed, passing on either side.

A fresh breeze came in through the top of the window, slid over the hands, the neck, and the damp forehead.

Along the shore below, long white waves emerged from the foamy mist, surged over the flat rocks, lost their shape, flooded in all directions, filtered into holes, receded, rose again, swept over the rocks, exploded into sheaves of foam.

More cars passed on both sides, trucks, bicycles. The people turned their heads, looking surprised.

I had a terrible time getting the motor started again.

Cars pass, Indian file, trucks, bicycles...

Perez is still sitting on the bench, legs apart, arms stretched at shoulder height along the bench back. His head is etched precisely into the left corner of the window, and also into the corner of the left window pane, that is hinged perpendicularly to the window frame. The curtain hangs at a slight angle, exposing a fragment of sidewalk and street. Mirror images glide over the glass, which should permit unobserved observation. However, that is not certain.

Perez is staring at his feet. He has lighted a cigarette, he is exhaling little puffs of smoke. He leans forward and spits the stub into the gutter...Leans back again, crosses his legs, watches the coming and going of cars for a moment...Pulls another cigarette from his trouser pocket, lights it, inhales, scratches his neck, stretches out his arms...

Raises his head...

The sudden vast glistening brightness makes the eyes blink. The glare is overpowering: the lids close, the throat tightens, blood mounts to the head, the temples pound rapidly.

The light floods the room, slams against the bare wall opposite the window, against the drawer of the night table, against the arms of the chair, the foot of the bed, slides over the patterns in the red wool rug, over the grey cotton bedspread, hits the bookcase at an angle, the gold-stamped bound volumes, runs along the ochre-colored varnish on the perfume burner in the corner of the shelf, stumbles against the chair legs in the other half of the room, against the table, the alarm clock, the black plastic telephone, the doors of the wardrobe, slants across the large lavendar rectangle tacked to the wall above the table, shedding light on a maze of roads, countless alleys, dead ends and ramified detours: on the map of the old city.

Only the white stone chandelier resists the onslaught: an impervious dull finish protects the smooth surface from glistening, from all fleeting luster.

From time to time the brief, clear clicking of the iron *Bocce* balls running into each other comes in through the open window, and the shouts of the players, when the traffic is not too loud.

Four of the eight alleys are being used, the four nearest to the bar. Several players are forming a circle around one of them, motionless they lean forward, eyes riveted to the ground, suddenly they get excited, shout accusations, claims and counter-claims, gesticulate wildly. After a while a short, pot-bellied man comes out of the bar, walks across the full length of the club grounds, asks the players to step aside, bends down, squats, spreads his hands out flat in front of him --to measure something; or to keep his balance--, straightens up again, says a few brief words, turns around, walks away. Order returns. At the other end they're throwing the jack: an arm stretches, falls back to the side...The small wooden ball runs, parallel to the wooden dividers, traces a shallow furrow in the sand. But that is, of course, not visible from this distance.

The young employee is still sprinkling the lawn. He has moved the tripod a little toward the center of the grass along the brick wall. He must have closed the spigot a little, because the water seems no longer to fall on the sidewalk of the avenue.

A group of cyclists arrives at good speed, followed by a bus, a truck, more bicycles...

Perez' eyes are cast down. He is consulting an appointment book on his knees...Writes something. Closes the book, slips it into his trouser pocket. Scratches his nose.

He stretches out his arms...

Black dots, black and white silhouettes go by, pale green reflections, grey ones, purple dots, shiny ones...The clouds have darkened. From silver grey, watery and translucid, they have turned a duller grey. Unnoticed curves appear, slightly in relief, perceptible with a wrinkling of the lids. The water surface is also darkening; the wind is dispersing sheaves of foam scooped away from the crests of the waves. Still, the accentuation into relief is not very clear, and the different effects of the two elements, now that both have grown darker, is perhaps due merely to the persistent blackish impression left on the retina by the asphalt of the avenue.

Besides, the fog veil is re-forming, hiding the waves; the entire shoreline, the open sea under its heavy leaden cloud ceiling, are once more bathed in the same uncertain light.

Down at the shore, slightly over two miles distant, rise the blocks of new houses, built for the relocation of the inhabitants of the old *mellah* --five parallel rows of houses running helter skelter along the shore, each storeway painted a different color. Behind them runs the ocean drive, in turn separated from the shore by a pebble path for pedestrians, an unbroken white fence and low tamarisk hedge planted at regular intervals along the embankment.

The embankment rises at the very edge of the rocks --a vast plateau of eroded slate, furrowed by a myriad of funnels, water holes, sharp-edged fissures, which the ocean has turned into an immense plain of motionless waves, crests, whirlpools, petrified eddies.

Without a moment's hesitation I turned around.

The big Buick was no longer in sight. It must have kept on going, or else it had stopped a little farther down the road: two or three hundred yards farther down, where metallic surfaces --chrome-plated; tin-plated-- reflected the sun; a constant sporadic contradicting shimmering that made it very hard to recognize any specific form or color; recognizing a car was out of the question.

Perez and Marietti had probably pulled off there and were sitting motionless side by side in the front of their old outmoded vehicle, its motor idling, their eyes on the road --one peering through the rear window, left elbow on the back of the seat, the other leaning out the door, his right hand still on the wheel, watching all three lanes of the road.

They must have stood watch all afternoon on Marine Boulevard, their car parked along the embankment or, more likely, along the curb of the traffic island in the center, in the shade of the palms, in spite of the no-parking signs there; they must have waited there all afternoon --for the little Fiat to wind its way through the maze of alleys, to emerge suddenly out of rue des Savetiers, float slowly out from under the archway, the light blue rectangle of the hood coming gradually into view, carefully skirting the dilapidated brick pillars; spent all afternoon waiting for the blue spot to appear on the deep red backdrop of the arch, killing time meanwhile, reading the paper, shaking off their drowsiness, smoking cigarettes, constantly scanning the embankment.

Although they had no reason to sit there all afternoon and keep watch: all they had to do was be there at six o'clock, a few minutes before six at most. Why so much zeal all of a sudden, when they had not made their presence known either on the way to lunch, or at the return to the Office, after lunch?

Perhaps they had just happened to drive by --or taken a ride just in case, ready for any eventuality...Besides, they may not have spotted the little Fiat before it turned into the ocean drive along the iron fences of the port, perhaps only at the very last minute, just as they were passing the wine truck...

Chance encounters are possible after all, coincidences, an unexpected crossing of ways...Although it is more likely that they were informed by someone at the Office, during the delay brought about by the interpreter. Because nobody, beside the chief, knew about the change in the working schedule made early that afternoon with his consent.

Somebody must have informed them on the spot, signalled an observer stationed close to the rue Fayard entrance, or in the alley outside the Office in the crowd that always waits around under the clerks' windows --or else informed them himself, run a couple of yards, made a phone call...

It takes only a minute of fast walking to reach the boulevard from the small side door to the Office, in the alley around the corner from the main entrance and, once on the boulevard, to signal an accomplice stationed along the embankment, or on the traffic island or, better still, in the Café des Alliés, on the other side of the traffic island, on the business side of the boulevard...

A telephone call from the Café des Alliés?...Not more than six or seven minutes can have elapsed between the car's departure from the courtyard and its arrival on Marine Boulevard: two to three minutes in the chief's office, one minute to back out of the garage, three minutes --counting generously-- to arrive at the boulevard through the maze of alleys.

One minute to reach the boulevard at a fast pace, another minute to telephone from the Café des Alliés, four to five minutes to drive to the spot...From Where? From another garage? From a café in the suburbs? From the shed outside the villa?

Someone must have alerted them. Saïd? Tahar, the interpreter? Ortiz, the accountant?

At the moment Tahar comes running out into the courtyard, Saïd is standing outside the garage door. Two or three minutes later he is still --or again-- standing in the same spot, in the same position. Meanwhile he is alone...

At a given moment, Saïd is alone outside the garage. It doesn't even occur to him to try running to the boulevard and back, since he can't know how long the conversation in the chief's office is going to take (what if it took only a few seconds, the time to answer yes or no?). He can do nothing more than try to tell somebody in the Office, accomplish an extremely simple step in an extremely short time, a series of rapid gestures inserted at the highest possible speed between his two identical poses at the beginning and at the end of the interruption.

Several other possibilities slip themselves immediately between the two identical silhouettes of the motionless Saïd, frozen into a single pose outside the garage door, possibilities that eclipse each other, succeed each other automatically in the almost tangible logic of sequence --the fluid continuation of movement: the rectangle of the courtyard which Saïd crosses diagonally, walking with long steps toward the offices overlooking the alley --Saïd, elbows pressed to his sides, running on the cobblestones in the alley-- Saïd's profile leaning into an open window toward another face veiled in shadow-- Saïd's torso pivoting outside the window --again the courtyard, crossed in the opposite direction-- and finally, Saïd "again" motionless outside the garage door.

And the same with: Tahar, alone in the corridor, pulling the door shut behind him --Tahar going back out into the courtyard, hurrying toward the alley-- Tahar running on the cobblestones in the alley --Tahar's profile, etc-- his torso, etc. --again the courtyard, the corridor --finally, Tahar pacing up and down the corridor, standing, placidly waiting for the conversation to end.

As for Ortiz...His office is next to the chief's; Ortiz sees everything that happens in the courtyard. Of course he can't telephone from his desk. Therefore he walks out into the courtyard, into the alley, toward the boulevard, to the Café des Alliés. He has plenty of time. He can justify his absence in a million ways. He can...But Ortiz isn't there this week. He went on vacation last Saturday...

Perhaps some other clerk...The registrar of vital statistics? The watchman? The mail clerk?...

Somebody --Saïd, Tahar, someone else-- informed them. At a given moment somebody crossed the courtyard, disappeared into the alley...

The incident --actual or imagined--, is barely one hour old and already it tends to abstract itself from its extremely short duration: severed from its ties to time, it will soon become isolated, stand out as a specific phenomenon, acquire the total, final density it will have from now on, a finished form which the memory will later recompose:

Somebody informed them. At a given moment somebody crossed the courtyard, disappeared into the alley, ran as far as the boulevard, told an accomplice, hurried back to the Office, back to his previous position.

Or else, just the opposite: Nobody informed them. They happened to drive by and spotted the car. (Or else:) Nobody had to inform them: that specific afternoon they kept watch on the boulevard and after a long wait, suddenly, they saw the car...

This is the form into which the facts will later be condensed, or into a similar form --an abstract, fluid recounting held together by the sole thread of the plot.

But the incident is still too recent. Scarcely an hour has elapsed...They probably sat there watching the boulevard or the ocean drive. They could just as well have kept watch outside the iron fences at the entrance to the port, in spite of the no-parking signs, anywhere along the waterfront...They would keep watch in the Office courtyard if they could, from behind the shutters, through the wooden slats; in the corridor outside the office; inside the office, if they dared.

At any rate, from whatever distance they had watched and noticed the car, they managed to get right behind it in the same lane, and pass it at their leisure, come extremely close and cut right across in front of it, rapidly diminishing the gap between themselves and the truck.

And now they were keeping watch down there, two or three hundred yards farther down the drive, peering through the rear window, through the open door, keeping an eye on all three lanes of the road, on every car that passed.

The same as this morning...

They were there first thing this morning, when the windows were opened with a single dry click, slowly detaching themselves one from the other, revealing the two-fold view of the avenue. The car was parked along the curb on the same side as the building, some fifty yards from the entrance, to the left. They sat motionless, they didn't talk, they· didn't smoke, they didn't raise their heads toward the roofs. They seemed to be staring straight ahead, unseeing, screwed onto the front seat, side by side, like two sawdust window dummies. They probably hadn't been there for more than a couple of minutes, perhaps they had stopped the car the very instant the window opened, but everything --their calm, their immobility, the dew on the fenders and the hood of the car-- seemed to suggest that they had been there all night, that they had spent the whole night dozing in that very same position, and just waked up, stiff and cold, not knowing what to do just then. Or else, they were still asleep, heads resting against the back of the seat, hands hanging, lifeless, on either side of their knees.

It was just seven o'clock. The blind, hiccoughing its way up, had just uncovered wide horizontal strips of grey foggy landscape.

The opposite sidewalk, the section of asphalt visible through the curtains, the red tiles topping the brick wall, and the slate roofs of the club buildings were midday dry. But the lawn was damp with dew, the leaves of the flaming iris that bordered the lawn, the bougainvillias, the geraniums along the path, the creeper that was climbing up the wall of the bar, all shone with wetness.

One could not see beyond the nearest trees of the park. The peeling eucalyptus trunks and singed branches pierced the fog screens in places, blending into the curtain of the first row of trees. Disappeared again when the fog glided a few yards ahead, pushed by a gust of wind, grew agitated, then scattered and rose rapidly, as though inhaled, and fused with the higher layer that was floating over the city, through which zones of greater luminosity radiated here and there, widened and shrank, incessantly moving from one end of the dull grey blanket to the other.

The rest of the landscape remained hidden. A variety of fields, countless contrasting shapes, planes, verticals, static or in motion, were hiding behind the mass of flaky foam.

Behind the immense opaque veil lay the harbor, the old city, the park, the waterfront, stood the factories, ten-and-twenty-story buildings, the white cathedral with its Moorish carvings still visible for another couple of seconds.

The windows had been pulled open, slowly detaching themselves from one another, revealing a two-fold image of the avenue. The air was fresh as every morning at the moment of awakening, the thermometer stood between 64 and 68 degrees. The avenue was almost deserted: over an hour ago the dock workers had passed in tight packs, pedaling as fast as they could toward Spanish Square, Marine Boulevard and the main entrance to the port. It grows animated only a little later, when the offices open. At the moment, a few trucks were passing, half empty. A cart went by, a sand wagon drawn by a mule, a group of women on the sidewalk in front of the building walked with short fast steps toward Roosevelt Square, native women probably, barefoot, draped in dirty patched veils. They had crossed rue Watier at the corner of the building, stepped up on the curb, arrived at the level of a parked black car with two men inside, sprawled against the upholstery, inert, apparently still asleep, their heads on the back of the seat, hands dangling loosely on either side of their knees.

Perez and Marietti were already on the job...

Half an hour later the whole panorama changed. Every morning the fog cleared in a couple of minutes: lines formed on the vast smooth canvas that stretched from one end of the horizon to the other; blurred, far-away lines that soon affirmed themselves and were now outlining many-colored streaked surfaces, accented by pale hues. The bright zones under the cloud layer multiplied, expanded in all directions, and fused. The thicker layer that covered the shore was breaking up: long tails of fog had gone up, unmasking narrow strips of sky, from which beams of light were falling here and there on the city, slanting like searchlights, drawing attention to various specific, far-apart points, in no recognizable order: the terraces of a skycraper, a line of palms, a yellow wall in the old city, a freighter at the dock, a billboard, a pink hill in the southern suburb, a billowing circle of pale green. Soon the last strands of fog lifted, the whole ocean came through, the whole city, the harbor, the nave of the cathedral, rows of trees along the outer boulevards, the shore line, miles of shore line, of jagged rocks, eroded slate, miles of dunes, juniper on the crests of the dunes, beaches of grey pebbly sand.

An airplane had taken off from the airport, passed very low over the roofs, flown over the coast, climbed rapidly and headed toward the open sea, soon it became a tiny brilliant spot that disappeared into a cloud.

The avenue became animated. Men in jackets, with open collars, a briefcase in one hand, and women in print dresses or dark skirts and white blouses were hurrying toward the business districts. A boy came running down the sidewalk, a bundle of newspapers under one arm, shouting a headline, deforming the consonants of syllables. Perez had climbed out of the car: he was standing in the street, leaning against the car door, hands behind his back, he was smoking a cigarette, his eyes staring in the direction of the brick wall several yards of which were covered with chalk graffiti in Arab characters which he was perhaps trying to decipher. While Marietti had stayed in the car, still sitting in the same position, motionless, reading a newspaper on his knees.

It was time to leave for work, to go once more through the variety of gestures, brief acts and rapid zig-zags, to accomplish the morning routine that finally led to the Office: to take the revolver from the night table and slip it into the trouser pocket, to open the door, step out onto the landing, turn the key twice in the lock, walk down the seven flights, pass the janitor's booth, walk out the door with its wrought iron panels, step cautiously onto the sidewalk, glance quickly in all directions, step off the curb, walk around the little Fiat parked in front of the entrance, shove the key into the lock with the left hand, slide behind the wheel, place the revolver on the seat at right, under a newspaper that lies there always, put in the ignition key, start the motor, let it run slowly for a couple of seconds, watch the sidewalk out of the corner of one eye, scan the avenue, shift into first, check the small oval mirror, step on the accelerator, turn the wheel, extricate the little car from the line of parked cars, go a little faster, shift into second, drive down the avenue toward Spanish Square.

At the gates of the park the Buick had already appeared in the rear-view mirror, some thirty yards behind, exactly at the same speed, obviously not trying to pass, nor to come any closer. In this fashion it followed, always at the same distance --sometimes faster, sometimes slowing down, according to traffic conditions-- as far as Spanish Square where, like yesterday, it turned right instead of crossing the square in the direction of the old city, and disappeared into Boulevard de la Gare.

Like yesterday they had been satisfied to trail the little Fiat for the short stretch up to the edge of the old city, had turned off and disappeared into the business district, had disappeared for the rest of the morning.

And in the same fashion the Buick had appeared a little while ago at the beginning of the ocean drive, but this time it had come up at a good speed, passed in the third lane, come very close, veered over toward the truck, cut off the road, leaving the little Fiat no other alternative than to ram into it or jam on the brakes instantly, brutally.

The big car came very close. Its rear fender passed at an angle, less than a yard from the bumper...Its long black body emerged on the left: the radiator, the hood with its chrome trim, the front door with its window up, and Marietti's face pressed against the glass...

The image now recomposes itself which another, at the time more impressive, or perhaps only seen for a longer duration (was it the blue rectangle spinning to the right, getting dangerously close to the huge body of the truck?) had, up until now, overshadowed or which the previous sequence had, at any rate, eliminated: the image of the two men, the instant they appeared on the left, completely concentrated on the execution of their maneuver, so different from what they had looked a few seconds before --Perez clasping the wheel with both hands, bent slightly forward, with tense eyebrows: Marietti braced against the back of the seat, his cheek pressed to the window, lips half open, his eyes concealed behind his dark glasses...

They probably stopped a little farther down the drive,

The ocean liner that was passing the jetty a little while ago has taken a south-west course. It is now quite far off the coast. Its white hull --a tiny hyphen, still visibly undulating-- glitters every now and then in the middle of the neutral uniform vastness where nothing guides the eye, where no distinct line divides sky and water, only the presence of the ship imposing itself as one of the last still discernible, undeniable parts of the water --which comes as a momentary surprise because, without the ship, the eye would certainly have fixed the horizon at a lower line.

The shore is the first clearly distinct line, struck at a sharp angle by a hem of pale green fronds that accents the arc of the outer boulevards. The recently planted palms along Boulevard du Caire --which is closest to the shore-- show only in a few places, but the closer eucalyptus along Boulevard de Suez stand considerably higher than the roofs of the ocean front villas; only two or three tall apartment buildings besides, of course, the cathedral, break the smooth, even line that continues uninterrupted all the way to Roosevelt Square.

A few tufts of acacia and wild pepper mark more modestly the pattern of certain streets in the section bounded by boulevard de Suez, avenue du Port, and Wilson Park. But no trees shade rue Lamarck or the dirt path leading from it to the club entrance: the afficionados are obliged to walk to the gate under the blazing sun. Some ten players, each carrying a bag, approach at a slow heavy pace. One of them trips over a stone, hops aside to regain his balance, his foot paws up dust, a small grey cloud rises from under his soles; he stops, looks around, slaps his trouser leg with the flat of his hand, walks on, catches up with his partners at the end of the path. The gate is open: they file through, one after the other and, one after the other, they disappear in back of the restaurant.

Five of the eight alleys are occupied, but the clicking of the balls and the shouting sound less clear than before because the traffic on the avenue is heavier now, perhaps, and louder. Children are playing on the grass outside the locker rooms. At the other end of the lawn the sprinkler is still spinning at the foot of the brick wall, but farther to the left now, in the corner of the grounds; exactly behind Perez' wooden bench --although it cannot be seen from the sidewalk: the wall is a good ten feet high...

The bench is empty.

But Perez isn't far off: he is strolling up and down the sidewalk. His khaki trouser legs appear from under the acacia branches, followed by his white sweater... Perez is coming back toward the bench, he passes behind it without stopping, walks another few yards toward Roosevelt Square, disappears under the leaves... Reappears, walking in the opposite direction... Perez is taking a little stroll, thumbs in his pockets, his fingers tapping against his trouser seams. Perez is relaxing, taking it easy...

Across the avenue, Marietti is still sitting in the car; he has not moved.

It didn't take long to cover, in the opposite direction, that portion of the road which I had driven over a few seconds earlier, behind the moving van --the two or three hundred yards of straight road from the stopping point to the point where the outer boulevards branch off, at the entrance to the ocean drive. Returning to the Office was out of the question, the urgent errands pretexted to the Commandant were supposed to take the rest of the day. The only thing to do was to drive home to Avenue du Port as fast as possible.

Had they, themselves, been surprised by the suddenness of the maneuver? Were they parked too far off to have had the time to turn back or to make out precisely what was happening on the road? --Had they simply driven on, and not stopped?-- At any rate, at the moment of making the turn (an extremely sharp turn which the rounding-out of the sidewalk transforms into a wide semi-circle with a single arrow in the center, pointing south, bi-lingual, laconic, commanding: "All directions"), there was not a car in sight anywhere along the shore front which the oval of the rear-view mirror, in a rapid panorama, immediately replaced with the massive, somewhat bandy-legged reddish clay tower directly on the shore, the last outpost of the old city against the ocean.

Boulevard du Caire, with its triple ranks of palms --one row along each sidewalk, in the pink gravel, the third on the traffic island that divides the boulevard into two wide one-way strips-- runs straight for half a mile through a zone of open land with, here and there, corrugated tin shacks and mud huts that serve as tool sheds to gardeners in black *serouals* or blue-jeans who grow tomatoes or squash on tiny irrigated plots. Then come the modern buildings, four-to-five storey houses, already a few years old, with black dirt streaks down the rain-pipes and metal blinds, with cafés, groceries and cheap clothing stores on the ground floors. Then comes the first traffic light: at the Trois-Palmiers intersection. Farther on, the arc of the outer boulevards continues with Boulevard de Suez running slightly more east, sectioned by several other traffic lights representing virtually as many stops, or as many threats of stopping, since they're not synchronized --and if they were, it would mean driving at reduced speed.

A hundred yards before the Trois Palmiers the light turned yellow. Impossible to pass, unless one drove through it, but this was not the place for that kind of violation: a policeman stood in the shade, at the opposite end of the square.

Stopping was inevitable. It was five to five on the little dash-board clock... Several cars were coming up on the straight stretch of road in back, which the distant Moorish tower seemed to block completely: they were impossible to identify, all rolling in a group, as though unable to get away from each other, floating on a kind of lake surface produced by the reflec-tions of the asphalt. Suddenly the lake evaporated; the cars were coming closer; already they had passed the open land and were reaching the first stores.

The light turned green... Better to get off the outer boule-vards and cut across the park quarter with its narrow parallel streets, almost all one-way, but without traffic lights --rue Pasteur, rue Copernic, not much traffic at this time of day, rue Lavoisier, wider, lined with acacias, rue Lamarck which leads to avenue du Port, less than a hundred yards from the entrance of the building--, turn left on the avenue, then almost immediately right, into rue Watier, where the car had a chance to pass unnoticed, park along the curb behind a truck, run back to the avenue, around the corner of the building, hurry through the iron gate, casting a rapid glance in the direction of Roosevelt Square: the big Buick was slowly rolling down avenue du Port, approaching calmly, silently...

The elevator was there, its door open as if to make things easier. The sound of the brutally slammed door vibrated up the staircase, then the purring of the elevator, another brusque slam of the elevator door on the seventh floor, all echoed through the building and throbbed heavily up the metal rods, soon followed by the sharper, almost insignificant slam of the door of the room, immediately choked by the pressure of hands, arms, shoulders flattening against the wood.

I leaned against the door, facing the wide open window, and stayed that way, motionless, for a few seconds, heart pounding, legs wobbly, forehead dripping with sweat, the few seconds it takes to catch one's breath.

A fine pale dust glitters from one end of the horizon to the other; a greyish mist veils the vibrations of the air and the rippling of the water. Sky and sea are fused into an undivided translucid substance, the color of lead. The transition from one element to the other is imperceptible. No dividing line can yet be seen; everywhere the same filtered light with its raw, blinding glare.

Farther below, the terraces of the old city form a network of uneven rectangles, joined one to another like panels of a mould. Wash is drying on the terraces; hundreds of pieces of cloth flap in the wind.

Closer, in the center of Wilson Park, the palms barely move. Only the high eucalyptus fronds on the edges are swaying.

Still closer, practically alongside the trees, stretch the grounds of the *Bocce* club, clasped between park and avenue: on the left, the roofed structures --bar, locker rooms, restaurant--; on the right, the alleys --eight long rectangles of ochre-colored earth, separated by low wooden dividers. Seven of the eight alleys are now occupied: the players gesture, argue, wipe their foreheads, change places with slow steps. Several have gone into the bar.

The clock over the locker rooms says six.

PART II

Six o'clock...

Always, everywhere, the same white light, the same glaring sky. Every day...

Yesterday.

Today...

Here, summer drags, uniform, without a clear outline, with no definite curve, it declines imperceptibly, has spurts of resurrection, invades several unprogrammatic months, lasts two seasons.

With the beginning of April the heat moves in. May is misty, humid; June bone dry; July sweltering, with showers and brief thunderstorms. However, at the beginning of July the temperature dropped twenty degrees, a cool wind blew in from the ocean, a belated spring wind that scattered the clouds, swept up sand and dust. But a couple of days later the heat was back, the damp heat, the lead-colored sky, the thin-spread slanting, blinding light.

As though summer were forever starting over again, all over again with each day: between eight and nine o'clock the heat pours in, accumulates; decreases only toward nightfall.

The nights are cool, almost chilly. The fog comes floating, filters in, piles up. Last night...

Every night.

Yesterday, Sunday... The same blinding sky, the same shimmering water, the same diffused, invisible sunlight; already the same maneuver of the two men on the avenue, after an hour's watch. The car was parked slightly to the left of the stoop, only the front shining through the thick acacia branches: the tarnished radiator grill, the fenders, the black hood with its flaking paint and, instead of the windshield (the whole car looked as though it had been rescued from a junk yard), the steering wheel, the dashboard and part of the front seat. One could even see the driver whom the reflection of the sky in the glass would ordinarily have hidden at this angle.

A few minutes before six Marietti sat up, as though suddenly awakening (as though he were ashamed of his long nap, finally ready, in a burst of energy, to execute the second phase of a program that had been meticulously planned in advance, a program which his more concientious colleague had all the while loyally continued to carry out), he rubbed his eyes, edged over to the other side of the seat, behind the wheel, started the motor, drove off in the direction of the port; a few minutes later he came back, at a leisurely speed. He couldn't have gone very far, probably no farther than the intersection in front of the park gates. He parked the car along the opposite curb, very close to the bench on which Perez was continuing his watch, a cigarette hanging from his lips, nose raised sky-ward, attentive and discreet. Both stayed there until nightfall, in placid silence, barely moving.

The circumstances were ideal for a repetition of yesterday's maneuver. Day and hour were propitious, the risks of failure very slight, and what did they risk, besides wasting their time, an hour or two of fruitless waiting, time which was lost for them anyhow, no matter where they did their waiting, on a bench along the waterfront, in a sidewalk cafe, in an armchair in the foyer of the villa...

Their information came from a reliable source. They knew that, if they appeared on Sunday, some time during the after-noon, they were more or less certain of not going to all that trouble for nothing, that, if they stationed themselves on the avenue at the same time as the day before, they'd have every opportunity to carry out their maneuver exactly under the same conditions and with the same effect, thereby endowing their activity with an air of continuity apt to impress the enemy or, at least, to impress him with the determination and tenacity which they intended to demonstrate.

Therefore, at precisely the same hour, they took up the kind of casual, patient, tenacious watch again which they had started Saturday afternoon, as soon as they had been alerted, as soon as one of their men at the Office --Ortiz, Tahar, or someone else-- had given them the word.

But their return this evening had seemed out of the question. Nobody would have expected it. Nobody would have thought of it. Monday always means large crowds at the Office; the work doesn't let up all afternoon. It's usually six before the courtyard clears, before the lines thin out, before the last cases (the most tenacious, endlessly rehashing the same old insoluble quibbles and, consequently, the most skeptical, finally, about the outcome of the arguments which they periodically revive) begin to leave, shaking their heads, half satisfied and half reproachful, walking down the front steps one by one, just when the shadow of the mosque, expanding eastward rapidly, would make their waiting bearable at last, allow for a pleasant nap at the foot of the high white wall.

Saïd is pacing the courtyard with tiny steps. He has put the office back in order, swept up, opened the windows, locked the door to the corridor; now he is walking up and down, hands clasped behind him, back and forth between stoop and garage, discouraging the dawdlers with a headshake, making them turn about with a single word:

-Tomorrow!

They'll all be back tomorrow, well before nine o'clock, waiting in two lines along the wall of the mosque, white *djellabas* and colorful shawls gesticulating in the sun outside the window, brilliant black eyes, motionless --in the slit between the veil of their *gandouras* pulled down over the fore-head and the silk kerchief pulled up to the root of the nose--, motionless at either end of a rectangle of brown skin --in turn framed, more or less at an angle, more or less animated, by two slats of the shutters--, exposed to that fresh sideway glance in which the protected eye may indulge with impunity... They'll all be there: the inveterate claimants, the new ones, the inspec-tor in the late morning, only too ready to promise the Comman-dant anything, to bury the incident, rather inclined to believe, from experience, that it will all work out, although quite worried about the turn events have been taking and the serious disagreements in the Office as to the measures to be adopted --disagreements which the Commandant has surely not failed to point out to him in the course of their Saturday afternoon discussion, if only to expose fully the consequences of his clumsiness and the amount of effort he was now obliged to make in order to conciliate his assistant.

But for the moment the office is empty, and much earlier than usual. Several new elements have come into the picture, a tangle of contradictions, a whole combination of circum-stances in the margin of routine: the steadily growing convic-tion that a trustworthy person should, at all cost, be put in possession of the facts; the plan, decided upon in the late morning, to contact L...for this purpose as soon as possible; the abrupt decision, taken after lunch, to go to see him before the end of the day; the departure from the Office in the middle of the afternoon; the premature interruption of the expedition (Had Perez and Marietti dreamed up their risky ocean front maneuver only to demonstrate that it was futile to try to quit the game, that they always accomplished their mission, no matter how, no matter what someone else might plan or intend to do?); the immediate giving up, the U-turn, the retreat to Avenue du Port --several small factors, one piled on top of the other, aggravating each other and also, most likely a misin-

The clocks struck six quite a while ago, but Marietti hasn't moved. He is still sitting in the car, inert, apparently staring at the trunk, the spare tire, or the license plate of the small red sedan that has just parked in front of him. He scratches his nose, his thigh, drums on the wheel; from time to time he stretches his legs sideways on the imitation leather seat...How much longer is he going to stay in that position, another few minutes, another hour, before joining his colleague on the other side of the avenue, or will he stay that way until it's time to leave? Do they intend to stay that way --Perez very properly seated on the bench, Marietti sprawled out all over the seat-- until the theoretical moment of lifting the siege, or are they planning to leave much earlier today, considering the demonstration sufficient?

The question --as well as the answer-- is no longer of any importance. Didn't they themselves just trace the true limits of their action, during the last hour? Nothing and nobody stopped them from mounting the stairs, the risks were practically nil, and they did nothing of the sort. Now the opportunity is lost: the super will come home any minute, so will the tenants on the sixth floor. Besides, if they had really wanted to get it over with, they would have tried yesterday afternoon when everybody was gone and the building was practically deserted until at least seven o'clock. They didn't even come near, except as a trick, walking up to the entrance at about six thirty, stepping up on the sidewalk, disappearing a few minutes into the entrance...But that was only a trick, they came back almost immediately, after standing briefly in the hall.

The whole business is nothing but a series of tricks, of practical jokes: Perez apes the dare-devil racing driver, eyebrows raised too high, eyes staring too wide, rolling his shoulders as though putting all his weight behind the execution of a forever inconclusive parody. Marietti, huddled in the corner of the seat, exaggerated tension written on his face, one pale cheek pressed against the window, follows the development of the S-turn with a knowing expression, but the proximity of the also mobile obstacle, or just his dark glasses, must blur the slightly exaggerated perfection, the too obvious, misplaced --in one word: useless-- casualness.

Perhaps it was really just a joke, improvised on the spur of the moment, and they had not quite realized the consequences. And now they've been moping around on the avenue for an hour, instead of trailing calmly... No, no: to have kept on driving, out of the traffic, riding on the empty highway, returning at nightfall with the knowledge of those two constantly in back, watching, would have been contrary to all common sense, contrary to the most elementary reflex of prudence.

Let them hang around there until tomorrow, if they feel like it, stretched out on the bench, squatting on the curb or on the front steps. Tomorrow morning will be time enough to spot them again, to see them just waking up, stiff and sore and grumpy . . .

The alarm will ring at seven, the room will grow bright, the blind will hiccough its way up, revealing successive horizontal bands of the usual fog-grey landscape. The windows, tugged open, will separate slowly, revealing the double image of the avenue below: the acacias, the brick wall, the deserted street, the tiny yellow stones that pave the sidewalk, the large black car parked along the curb --or else merely, as during all the previous months-- a line of cars along each curb, visible for some hundred yards on either side, cars of all makes, of subdued or strident colors, but no old outmoded black Buick anywhere...Perhaps they're not coming back, either tomorrow or the day after; perhaps they don't intend to push their demonstration too far; three days ought to suffice in most cases, the normal duration of a first warning, based on previous experience, according to the proportion of effective results.

A few days of intimidation are usually enough to impose silence, to discourage any activity contrary to their designs. If not, they immediately proceed to the second stage of their operation, which is simple and direct: machine gun fire at close range, a bomb under the car, firing into lighted windows at night. And later, in cases of exceptional stubbornness... Certain recent examples leave no doubt as to their determination, the precision of their weapons, and the constant impunity they enjoy...

Two black cars appear out of the shadows, headlights off, rolling slowly down the empty boulevard, one sixty feet behind the other. A man comes out of his house, lets the door slam behind him, takes a couple of steps on the sidewalk. The first car approaches, a blast of machine gun fire, the man sways, sinks to his knees. The car passes him, picks up speed, drives off as fast as it can. The wounded, kneeling man is holding his stomach, lifts his head, tries to cry out. A window opens in a nearby house, another window lights up. The second car approaches, another blast: the wounded man collapses; an arm gestures on the sidewalk, rises up...The arm falls back, the car drives past, flees at top speed, vanishes.

The fingers barely move, the nails scratch the pavement, the pebbles, the small yellow stones of the sidewalk torn up by the bullets, chunks of bark which the bullets have torn off the trees and scattered. The eyes close, the light of the street lamp blinks, fades, faints away.

A window opens, a second window lights up, a door squeaks, several windows light up, a door slams, the windows open wide, light up, all the doors open, slam, all the windows light up...

A brusque gesture sets the windows in motion. They pivot slowly, slowly they swing toward each other, immediately blotting out large peripheral sectors of the field of vision, wiping out symmetric lateral strips, two at a time: the hills in the southern suburbs and the factories in the north, the suburbs and the docks of the port, the cathedral and the sky scrapers, two lines of trees at the outskirts of the park, two opposing sections of the old city. Like a scroll, whose suddenly released ends rapidly roll toward each other, until only a narrow gap is left in the middle, with a few last scrawls still visible, bits of curves and incisions, the landscape shivers, sways and gradually sinks, drowned in the folds of the curtain, soon shrunk to a vertical furrow, a crack through which peek lawn, terraces and sunlit green, the shore, the ocean, the sky on top with its blinding glare piercing silver grey clouds.

The two window panes are only a few inches apart. A second brusque gesture makes them tremble, snap into one another.

The handle squeaks as it turns.

The curtains shook for a moment, now they fall straight, motionless, across the full width of the bay window. Beyond them, far beyond, lies a blur of broken lines, confused distorted shapes, dull colors, all uniformly veiled with grey and gold, all fused into each other, unidentifiable. It would take sharper, more accurate eyes, more alert, better trained, a much wider span of vision to tell them apart.

The room is now isolated, cut off from the outside world. The light is less glaring than before, but still very bright. It seems to ooze out of the walls, the ceiling, the curtains, as though from a new, independent source. The sounds from the avenue come in muffled, or rather, there are no sounds at all during the first few minutes. Everything falls silent suddenly, drawing one's attention retroactively to the noise that had not stopped until then, the memory of which grows hollower, unravels itself, molds itself to the very proportions of silence. Soon after the sounds start afresh, mount again, although fringed with secondary vibrations, distorted, almost unrecognizable: of all the motors snorting up and down the avenue, only that of the bus remains clearly distinguishable; a horn blows, but the sound is muffled and immediately interrupted.

An airplane appears, flies very low over the roof tops. Its purring makes the windows shudder. Rapidly it flies off toward the ocean, makes an arc above the shore, turns back toward the old city, passes over the old city, over the port...Becomes a shiny dot, a reflection from one of the propellers or a window in the cabin.

The reflection disappears.

The purr had been inaudible for a long time.

There is nothing more to see outside the window.

In the room, the silvery yellow light dappled with fine white grains seems to converge toward the center of the rug, toward the red wool patterns whose cubist motifs, four regular rows of irregular squares, cover the full length of the rug: silhouettes of horses, warriors, stylized weapons, lances, pikes, interplays of lines, triangles, circles, pacing off the short itinerary from one end of the room to the other, from window to door, from door to window, always the same straight stretch in the narrow aisle between table and bed.

At every step the revolver, which, up to now, had not felt heavier inside the trouser pocket than any other habitual object (as intimate and, therefore, as ignored a part of the daily routine as a ring of keys or a large handful of change), at every step the revolver beats against the leg, pulls at the fabric, unbalances the stride. Its weight becomes more and more noticeable, more and more irritating. Soon it feels unbearable.

It is a short-muzzle 38, light and easy to carry, perhaps not the most accurate, but practical and simple to handle. There are a couple of rust stains on the butt; a few grains of tobacco have gotten stuck to the trigger and the safety. A thread of oil is oozing out all along the barrel with --to guarantee prompt, effective return of fire-- the first bullet permanently in place.

Lying on the night table, between the lamp and the ceramic ash tray, it looks like a toy which copies the adult model in every detail --sights, clip, stamping on the butt--, but usually its true purpose is betrayed by shininess. This one would be a dirty toy, worn, tarnished by salt water and much handling.

The revolver leaves the night table in order to plunge into the trouser pocket, from which it emerges only to go into the desk drawer, the middle drawer that is kept slightly open, the grip always ready for the reaching hand. If necessary, one only has to bend the forearm: the fingers let go of the fountain pen, immediately find their position, the thumb on the safety catch, and the index on the trigger. The operation requires no other gesture: the left arm, chest, head, legs, the rest of the body, remain motionless.

It may happen that the revolver isn't in any of the afore-mentioned places. In that case it is at the end of the extended arm, loaded, ready for immediate use. But these moments are brief, if not rare, and it's on the night table, after all, that it stays most of the time, practically half the time, all night at any rate, sometimes joined by the phone, between the pale blue lamp and the ochre-varnished ashtray.

All night long, at regular intervals, the beam of the light-house projects the shadow of the window onto the walls of the room, the shadow of the white stone chandelier, the shadow of the perfume burner on the shelf, and onto the white wall over the bed, the shadow of the lamp and of the black bakelite telephone. Later, after the blind has been pulled down, forms and colors disappear; the metal surfaces no longer glitter here and there: the knob on the table drawer, the lock and latch on the door, the cradle of the receiver and, all the way back, on the right of the wardrobe, the handle of the bathroom door. Sometimes, when the light goes on in the hall, a yellowish streak falls across the floor.

Without the telephone the three objects compose a well-balanced still-life in harmonious, subdued colors on the wooden, slightly dusty background of the table.

Everything seems calm outside the door. Not a sound mounts the stairs, no rhythm of footfalls, no furtive scraping on the imitation marble steps, no unconscious stubbing of a shoe tip against the banister spindles. All is quiet...

The bathroom door squeaks slowly open, revealing the small frosted-glass window through which falls a white milky light --a light one finds in hospitals or in the washrooms of a big hotel--, and directly under the window the sink.

Soon water spurts from the two wide open faucets, hot at first, then lukewarm, suddenly ice cold, freezing the fingers which were testing the temperature under the stream. The hands plunge into the pale-rose-tinted liquid, draw back at once, take hold of one another, clasp each other, plunge in again, continue to clasp, wriggle in a splashing of foam and bubbles, as though forcing each other to dunk, waging a brief, brutal war against each other in the dirty water --as if they were going to fight until one of them let go, stopped moving suddenly, wavered, slowly sank to the bottom and lay there, inert, open, floating motionless, lifeless.

The sink empties out in a thunderous gurgle that has no apparent relation to the amount of liquid that is escaping, followed by hiccoughs, grumbling, dull thuds echoing in the pipes. Drops have fallen on the small table, on the towel rack, on the strip of linoleum, on the imitation sandstone floor, all the way to the threshold of the room. No need to take precautions: the room has neither parquet nor carpeting, wet feet won't hurt the rug.

The door closes. There is one brief whistle, as if to complement the squeak that accompanied the opening, or its abridged repetition --a recapitulation of the sound motif, a mocking refrain.

Everything on the table has been laid out in the usual order: the desk blotter in the center, the candlestick on the right, behind the candlestick the alarm clock in its leather box as flat as a cigarette case, the letter paper on the blotter and finally, on the left, the telephone which one must not take off the hook automatically if it should ring --although it will probably not ring before tonight.

The fountain pen is in the table drawer, also the eraser, the envelopes, a scrap of blotting paper, a few short badly sharpened pencils and two black and white photo postcards, one a view of the *Palais de Justice* in the heart of the European city, with its turn-of-the-century colonial-style pediments and arcades, the other the Big Mosque in the new *Medina,* with its long windowless walls, its embrasures and its huge square bell tower.

The table is quite large, not especially beautiful, but sturdy and solidly braced against the wall, in front of the map of the old city. The chair is harder to balance, a bit rickety in most positions, except when one tips it slightly to the right, which has the advantage of turning away from the window: the light slants over the shoulders from the back and doesn't tire the eyes. These are the best writing conditions in this particular room.

Because the only thing to do is tell him everything in a letter, since it can't be done face to face. Although a meeting would have been preferable, writing is only a poor substitute. But the attempted meeting came to a sudden end; it ran into a major, totally unexpected obstacle from the very start and will probably not be possible now before next Saturday. Besides, there is no guarantee that L...will be at home Saturday afternoon, and he has no telephone on his farm...At any rate, too much time will have gone by before Saturday, Sunday. If he is to be told what happened, it must be now, and not at the end of next week.

L...would certainly have been there today: he is always there in the late afternoon. This very moment he is probably sitting on his terrace, wedged into his armchair, attentive, half sarcastic, half intrigued.

Now the only thing to do is write it all down as clearly as

possible, to explain it all to him as concisely as possible, without unnecessary detail, but without omitting anything essential. Or else to ask him to come to the Office during the week... Although, no, that would pose the same problem: he couldn't come before Saturday, he's busy all week on his property...

Sidi Rachid is a *douar* some six miles from Aïn Beida, at the end of a straight road that is usually in good condition, except when it rains --a straight road on a desert-like pebble plateau, furrowed by wide muddy rivers after a thunderstorm... The place is mentioned on the map, two words in tiny letters, a thin line drawn through a brown dot...

The map of the old city hangs behind the table, smooth and flat, unsmeared by fingers, unbent, untorn, carefully fastened to the wall with a dozen golden-headed tacks. It is a large linen-paper rectangle of a lavender shade, approximately a yard wide and a yard and a half high with, in the center, an irregular, not readily definable shape roughly resembling an isoceles triangle pointed north-east, with the Moorish tower standing on the beach at the entrance of the water front as its tip, and the south-west north-east course of Marine Boulevard as its perfectly straight base. But the other two sides of the triangle are far less symmetric: the line along the port forms a feebly billowing sinusoid and the other --from Spanish Square to the Moorish tower-- is broken up into five unequal segments. All three sides of the triangle are reinforced by a thick purple line that corresponds to the old earthen ramparts (a frank red in certain spots, in others an indefinite color between dirty grey, pink and pale yellow) that run all the way around the city, cut by the one-way arches which are the only exits from the tangled alleys of the center. Which had perhaps in former times --seen from the open sea, or the distant plains-- looked like a real fortress city, isolated on the shore, away from any neighboring settlements, its walls dominating the wave-beaten rocks on one side and the stony naked soil on the other, overgrown with jujube bushes and fichi d'India. Today it lies squeezed between the port and the modern sections, dominated on all sides by metal scaffolding, cranes, apartment and office buildings. Around the old wall the open space has shrunk to a couple of yards, four or five yards in the regular streets, ten or so on Marine Boulevard with its tall palms along the traffic island reaching up to the embrasures. On the sidewalk at the foot of the old wall, artisans offer their home-made wares to the tourists --copper, iron, leather, wood-- and curse the slump: the crisis is at its worst, visitors stay away. There is a kind of "flea market" behind the ramparts where you can buy anything at extremely flexible prices. L...lost his wallet there, the last time he took a walk in the *Medina*. That was over a year ago, before it all started.

It would of course have been simpler to tell him the whole thing, to have a quiet chat with him about it, if only to be able to explain one or two ambiguous details. On the other hand, in case of a mishap, a letter would certainly be more solid proof than a single oral statement, at that point already reduced to giving existence to prior, by now unverifiable testimony. Why let anybody in on the secret, if not for the sole purpose of making these revelations, if need be, to the largest possible and least dismissible audience, for the public re-establishment of the truth? Because one could always find some agency to furnish a distorted, incomplete or erroneous account of the facts, not that the initial reports actually concealed them, but in most cases they were kept only as source material for more satisfactory write-ups, simplified, corresponding more to the official concept...

It had happened on a Sunday morning, a few weeks before the beginning of the events. He had gone for a walk through the *Medina,* out of curiosity. He hadn't gone back there since. Nobody ventures any more beyond the old walls, unless forced by one's job or prompted by a taste for danger.

A maze of narrow alleys and dead-end streets --themselves divided and ramified-- stretches over a mile beyond the walls, roofed passages, blind alleys, small squares and intersections of all imaginable shapes, triangles mostly, that seem to owe their existence solely to the chance meeting of three zig-zagging alleys in quest of an outlet. On the map it appears as a tangle of straight, curved and broken lines forming, against the pale lavender paper, a variety of polygons, streaked with thin horizontal parallels of a firmer, darker print. These shapes correspond to the built-up areas and are, for the most part, so complex that the attention is first drawn to the few rectangles and squares toward the east of the city, to the section near the port where the foreign consulates established themselves at the beginning of the century. The rest is an array of highly complicated cut-outs that fit more or less into one another, although separated everywhere by tiny intervals, like pieces of a puzzle that one had understood, but not bothered to put together. These "blank" spaces --some straight-lined corridors of unchanging width, others of various shapes, wider in one point, narrower in another-- compose, at first glance, a totally irrational network of arteries or, at least, totally contrary to all principles oridinarily derived from rationality, such as efficiency, simplicity, economy. It is as though it had all been planned in order to obstruct movement to the utmost, to block traffic, defy convenience and enjoyment, sabotage civic surveillance, hamper pursuit, favor disorder and anarchy. These streets do not seem traced to facilitate coming and going, nor any need to reach the dwellings. No intention whatsoever seems to have inspired their layout --they don't actually seem to have been "laid out". They look more like the product of empirical machination, as though all the spaces spared by successive random constructions had been assembled end to end. In many places the vacant space has been reduced to less than an inch, which the surrounding buildings seem only too ready to swallow up completely, their horizontal lines practically reaching out to join. What could happen if this contempt for movement were pushed to its extreme? The few inches of free space between the housefronts would disappear completely, people would have to squeeze sideways through dark, evil-smelling corridors, to go from one house to another through the windows of the corresponding storeys, to get from one section to another by leaping from terrace to terrace, across from one end to the other of the whole dense, sordid, impenetrable agglomeration. As it is, the tiny alleys stand out on the vast triangular surface traversed by parallel lines at neat intervals, like the cobweb-fine veins of an ivy leaf.

But there is another way of looking at it. The way one can consider a relief map either as the description of a mountain chain cut through the plains, or as an exceptionally mountainous plain, one can regard the map of the old city not as representing blocks of urban dwellings on a uniform background of virgin land, but rather as the minute reproduction, on a built-up background, of an extraordinary combination of thoroughfares. And immediately, in a flash, the map makes sense and comes to life: dozens of mobile lines, launched from the periphery, plunge in all directions into the compact mass of structures, divide it, chop it up, skirt the isolated blocks, draw loops around them, split them with diverging tributaries, continue the infiltration into the remotest sectors, escape behind the city walls, snoop into the narrowest corners, return toward the center finally, go back to their starting points. It is a dense, complex communication system that leaves the city open to every wind that blows, abandons it unreservedly to constant crushing traffic. Every single point looks rapidly accessible, every section has been admirably served. A number of itineraries outline themselves; two or three stand out right away, because of their clear straight course, very much like the rivers in models which seem either peaceful or torrential, according to the illusion created by a few luminous lines. But in most cases these distinctions are difficult to establish, or have to be revised almost immediately. The alleys keep changing width and direction, like high mountain paths crossing summits or plunging into ravines. Although here the alleys zig-zag on flat, perfectly even terrain: rue du Capitaine-Zeller starts to narrow from Spanish Square that one expects it to stop after a couple of yards; it hair-pin turns, practically runs back to its starting point, widens, reverts to its initial direction, heads a good way north, and finally leads into the ocean drive after having crossed the city from end to end. Rue Sidi-Boubkeur, on the contrary, starts out much wider at the wall and one expects it to continue all the way to the port, but it stops dead and fuses with rue du Capitaine-Zeller after only a hundred feet. At a short distance, a long narrow street runs parallel to the city wall, incorporates several blind alleys on either side, turns abruptly, collides with a building, becomes a dead end and disappears. Actually each street, no matter how narrow, serves a whole network of secondary alleys that sometimes run so far and in such unpredictible directions, that one ought to trace a line across the roofs and terraces in order to get the correct notion of the distance to be covered. In that way, one could see how a certain house on a certain street is, in reality, by the connection of a narrow, twisting blind alley, built on an entirely different, distant street; how two blind alleys that start in different places sometimes join, or at one point separated by a single *gourbi;* yet, to go from one to the other, one must describe a wide circle of larger streets, climb up and down a double hierarchy of alleys. Or an alley may suddenly branch off, plunging the stranger into perplexity; but then the truncated ends merge again behind a building a few yards ahead and put an end to the unnecessary dilemma.

At any rate, this geography of narrow streets and blind alleys, this system of thoroughfares and compulsory passages is, in practice, to a large extent disturbed, sabotaged even, by the intervention of elements of a different nature, elements that rebel against classification and cannot be indicated on a map, even if it were drawn to a still larger scale: balconies so close to one another that one only has to step over the railings to reach another section; roofed bridges suspended between two houses providing a rigorously in-group communication system; graded terraces permitting one to travel without obstacle at an easy height, and in the greatest secrecy, from one point to another, between which the coming and going of a patrol would make all communication impossible, or highly risky. The cellars and their underground extensions are further guarantees of secrecy.

Looking at dozens of these narrow, uneven, angular channels, with the knowledge that many hidden paths complete them and add to them, suggests --in spite of the restricted area within which they function-- an infinity of roads and passageways, straight or winding short-cuts, detours, outlets, bends, wrong turns, escape valves, way stations, new starts. Every time the eye shifts across these precise thin lines, every time the eye leaps forward in these winding alleys, new perspectives open, new routes appear. The scale of the map is ideal for this kind of slow parallel advance: every inch represents thirty feet, each tenth of an inch three feet-- a visual scale ideal for conscientious reading of a city for pedestrians.

Several symbols of different character break the uniformity of the horizontal streaks, staking out the phases of this exploration: shaded balls depict the trees of the municipal square, of the park around the port and Place de l'Europe; parallel verticals cross-hatched with fine lines indicate public buildings: the covered market, police headquarters, the public health service; slanting parallels stand for religious edifices: seven mosques, three zaoïas, marabouts flanked by the Islamic crescent; crosses for the Catholic mission; small crescents for the tiny Sidi Othmane cemetery; filled-in squares grafted onto the purple lines for the nine towers in ruins that stand against the city wall, four facing the port, four facing the plain, and the ninth, on the rim of the port, facing the plain and that part of the shore near the north-west tip of the city.

The waterfront starts at that point, as the theoretical continuation of the ocean drive, and Boulevard de Suez, a little farther off, with its two traffic lanes in either direction and the median that divides them in the center, using up, by itself, the width of several alleys; if it had been cut through the old *Medina,* one fourth of the buildings would have had to be demolished. The unaccustomed eye is taken by surprise as it speeds down the vast sweep, repeating in the opposite direction and on the other side of the walls the difficult itinerary that had led from Spanish Square to the waterfront and that now leads into the European city, where it reverts to modern regularity, to luxuriously straight lines, solely inspired by utility, based on a notion --and a utilization-- of space which seems over-simple after the recent excursion into the Moslem section. The European city is the section for trucks, busses, many-colored sidestreets with pedestrian crossings, traffic lights, white lines marking the lanes, route signs and traffic signals at every intersection. Completely unlike the *Medina,* with its white-barred red discs at the beginning of every one-way street, putting an end to not knowing which street to enter. Scooters, bicycles, hand-drawn carts all obey the signs; the risk to which the violator exposes himself --suddenly face to face with a patrol-- is far greater than the pleasure of disobedience.

The patrols guard the city day and night, walk back and forth and around a varying number of times during their six-or eight-hour shifts; each patrol has its own beat --rue du Port to Place de l'Europe, rue Moulay-Idriss, rue Pierre-Bous-selle, rue du Dar-el-Askri, rue du Port to Place de l'Europe, rue Moulay-Idriss..., sometimes two patrols meet at the crossing points of two beats, walk a short stretch together, separate, lose sight of each other, meet perhaps a second time during the night, each slowly strolling through its net-work of alleys, each conscientiously inspecting the assigned sector, poking into the remotest dead ends, hurrying in the approximate direction of an explosion, a whistle, a call for help. The contrast is great between the sight of these alleys full of uniforms, practically empty after nine p.m., and the dense milling, the general lightheartedness that reigned there in former days, before the events, before the Commandant's map began to be studded with tiny blue, red, green or black crosses.

The top sheet of the letter pad is still blank, except for the date in the upper left corner: Monday, August thirteen. The letter remains to be written, an understandable synopsis of the last three days to be put into words. But is it not to be feared that the recipient, thanks to one or more optic delusions, will not realize its full import? Won't the contents be falsified from the start, if restricted to the present incident rather than preceded by a brief background? But in that case, how far should one go back in the sequence of facts? To last month's disturbances, to the different atmosphere that has existed ever since the establishment of the curfew, or all the way back to the beginning of the events? And even then?... Ought one not to go back to the initial campaign, to the days when the first scaffolding of the operation was being set up? Without going that far, it should be possible to trace a concise, accurate picture of the most recent developments, and what could be more convincing that the map of the city itself, studded with landmarks crayoned in every day for several months? What could be more eloquent than this canvas of many-colored crosses gradually invading the large lavendar rectangle, growing into garlands with the news of disturbances and their suppression?

Every evening, when the coming and going is over, the Commandant sits down at his desk and writes his report, then he stands up, with an assortment of crayons in one hand, faces the map on the wall and draws a small blue cross here, a green one there, a yellow one, a red one, a black one, according to the type of outrage or crime committed. Sometimes he hesitates, unsure of how to classify an incident, or tempted to mark it with several crosses when he judges it particularly important. During the first few months it even happened that there was nothing for him to mark for a week. But those days are far behind. Since then the crosses have multipled so much, that two or three spots can't hold any more: the Commandant squeezes them in as best he can, into the immediate neighborhood of these unlucky areas, into corners where, in actuality, nothing ever happened. Other, very rare sectors, on the contrary, have remained untouched, which now makes them look suspicious.

This superimposes a fourth order on the alleys and dead ends and one-way streets, on the terraces and clandestine passages, an order that may seem fortuitous with its scattered daily events, but whose outlines appear after a while, stand out, assert themselves. For the layman, all these crosses or identical size refer to acts of identical importance. Actually, some are milestones of special moments --the start of a new phase in the struggle, a spectacular ambush, the climax of a long period of tension.

But most of them represent only very ordinary episodes, a banal element of a well-established routine --like the two new crosses the Commandant drew in yesterday: the first behind the covered market, into a square where a public scribe had just been assassinated; the second at the north tip of the city, 17 rue Lalla-Sfia.

There, in the foyer of a prosperous-looking house, during the night from Saturday to Sunday, shortly before two a.m., a bomb exploded.

The violence of the explosion tears the door to shreds; they fly in all directions; pieces of beam, chunks of metal and plaster are blasted out into the street. The noise of the concussion echoes down the alley, all the way to the city walls, alerting the policemen who stand guard at Bab el Bahr, on the ocean drive-- at the same time alerting the patrol that walks around the municipal square; but at that moment the soldiers happen to be walking along the opposite side of the square, they are at the farthest possible point from the accident; besides, the acoustics is bad, leaves distort the sound; the patrol takes the wrong turn, loses precious time in a dead end. Consequently the policemen are first to arrive, in a jeep; disregarding the one-way sign; they stop at the beginning of the rubble, proceed on foot to No. 17, where they find two men in shirt sleeves with mussed hair and dust-smeared faces trying to clean up. The policemen enter the foyer, make the habitual inquiries; at this point a second jeep arrives, leaves again almost immediately in the direction of the ocean drive, circles the entire *Medina* on the outside, passes under the walls into rue Fayard, comes out in the Office courtyard.

The duty sergeant at the Office is informed of the incident. He jots down the essentials in a large record book; adds a few extra details, asks a couple more questions.

Glances at his watch...

It is almost two in the morning. The lighthouse intermittently illuminates the room. At regular intervals --eight seconds, six seconds, three seconds--, the beam of light that sweeps the coast bursts into the room, hurriedly projects the shadow of the window onto the walls (elongated crossbars, distorted latch, the mobile silhouette of the curtains, folds in the fabric, rapidly unfolded, refolded), the shadow of the candlestick on the table, the shadow of the perfume burner in the shelf corner-- and flees, leaving imprinted on the brain the image of those objects that had been briefly caught in the funnel of brightness. The first beam of light lasts the longest; the second is very brief, it merely brushes the walls; the third stays a little longer; during the few seconds following its appearance, the three luminous escaping streaks light up the sky above the old city, slide across the waves and describe a huge arc over the ocean, while the lighthouse itself is nothing but a tiny brilliantly clear red light. Then everything blurs again on the surface of the water; the three bright streaks have disappeared, turned toward the open sea. Several seconds pass. Suddenly the first beam reappears on the right, approaches the land, returns at top speed...

All is dark in the room, except for the table on which the lamp is projecting a cone of white brightness. The guard is writing the hour into the permanent record book, the time of the explosion, the time of the patrol's arrival at the Office; he mentions name and number of the squad who drove to the place, the exact location of the damaged building, the identity of its owner, the nature of the damage.

The patrolmen salute and depart. The sound of their jeep decreases as they drive away from the Office, vanishes as they turn the corner into rue Fayard.

The guard gets up, consults a typewritten sheet that is tacked to the wall, comes back, sits down again, scribbles a number on a piece of paper.

Takes the telephone off the hook...

The beam of light bursts into the room, illuminates the wall over the bed, projects the shadow of the window, of the curtains, of various objects abruptly torn from darkness come to life for the duration of a flash, greyish images that flee on the white screen of the wall.

Then all grows black again...

All grew black again. The telephone rang. The lighthouse illuminated the room for another brief instant...

The telephone rings (had it rung before?).

The room is completely black, except for a faint shimmer from the window side, probably because the blind has not been drawn.

Another shrill ring, just as the beam of light crosses the room, revealing the telephone within reach, the ashtray, the revolver, the pencil placed across the pad, the lamp, the plastic switch.

The darkness returns, but not for long: an instant later the lamp projects a funnel of brightness onto the sheets, the rug, the pillow, the night table, the telephone.

Soon, an extremely calm voice speaks at the end of the wire, spells out a number, the name of a street, a specific hour, while the tip of the pencil runs across the pad, scribbles a word, a figure, another word, a number, doodles figures, a cross, a circle, starts a triangle, draws a line.

It was five after two on the watch on the table. A pale light shone from the window. The blind had not been drawn. The night was black, the sky clear. At regular intervals the lighthouse illuminated the curtains, fled, swept over the old city (it was necessary to go there at once, to get dressed, to take the revolver, the car keys, to walk downstairs, through the hall and out the front door which is never locked, to drive off in the direction of the port, to stop on Spanish Square in response to the policeman's halt signal, to enter the old city through rue des Bouchers, drive through the whole old city to get to the scene of the "drama"), left the shore, swept over the waves, described huge circles above the ocean, disappeared toward the open sea. The lighthouse itself was nothing but a tiny red dot, shining feebly, far far away toward northwest, very feebly through the window panes, far away, behind the curtains.

The watch face says a quarter to seven. The light is still raw, but less glaring than a little while ago. Muffled sounds filter in from the avenue, as soon as the ear listens for them again. The curtains fall, straight and still, across the full width of the bay window. Broken lines shine through, confused, dismembered shapes, tarnished colors veiled in grey and gold, the colors of the clouds, perhaps, or of the ocean, or of that in-between zone which the eye cannot clearly discern --since it cannot plunge below the shore line, or go farther left than the cathedral (the chair is standing at the extreme left of the bay window, obviously pulled back); on the right, the range of vision stops abruptly at the traffic circle in the park.

The table wobbles once again, one leg taps the floor. Pushed back all the way against the wall, it again parallels the lavender margin of the paper, its edge running exactly under the map, where five straight arteries converge on the large rectangle of Spanish Square which is still not quite completed. Temporary medians for the regulation of traffic occupy the center of the square. The north side consists of the old city wall, pierced at one point, toward the middle, by a quarter-of-an-inch-wide breakthrough: rue des Bouchers. Farther up stretch the sections of the *Medina* in thin horizontal streaks; farther down a uniform pale lavender surface represents the asphalt and paved sidewalks of the square.

At second glance this surface is composed of an infinity of tiny grey and lavender dots, as though the printer had tried to portray every stone of the pavement. The fat purple line that runs around it, varies in thickness: it swells in places, shrinks in others, exactly like the old wall itself, which is an amalgamation of more or less dilapidated reddish ragstones, worn down by rain, more or less solidly put together, reinforced by recent layers of plaster and clay, especially at the entrance to the alley where cars and small trucks often bump into the wall and damage it; tufts of dry grass grow here and there in the chinks; the naked stones and pebbles hold together by sheer miracle, occasionally come loose and fall on the sidewalks, on either side of the narrow breakthrough --too narrow, actually, since the street is a good twelve feet wide at its start, lined by cleanly whitewashed or yellow ochre, grey and pale-blue rough-cast two-storey houses; only farther on it begins to shrink, at the first butcher shop; all the butcher shops are painted red, bright reds, violent reds, at night they're closed with wooden shutters and padlocked iron bars, or gates of a darker, almost brownish dull red that contrasts, in the beam of the lighthouse, with the glossy billboards and the shiny streaks which the street lamps (lamps with large metal reflectors, suspended every sixty feet by a cable from house to house, swaying in the wind) paint onto the metalwork of the doors; with the reflections in the puddles in the asphalt, with other darker, more fragmentary reflections of blood stains and scraps of left-over meat and garbage that litter the street and both gutters, investigated by hordes of cats that run off at the sound of the motor, dive into sewers, behind loosely closed shutters, under boards, boxes, buckets, garbage cans, or else flee in front of the car, a piece of black meat in their teeth; the wheels spin, slide, skid, splash through a puddle, the red shops glide by on either side, after some two hundred feet the alley turns at right angles (the surprised cats panic, throw themselves under the car) curves, widens, leads into Medersa Square, with its grey tile pavement, becomes rue Sidi-Fettach which continues rue des Bouchers on the other side of the square, a winding, narrow, completely

top of the other, take a dramatic turn, it's always better to see for oneself, on principle, to show one's face).

One of the doors led to a slightly larger room furnished with pallets all around the walls, with cushions and carpets, lighted by a candlestick on a small high table. A musical instrument, that resembled a mandolin, lay abandoned in one corner. A teapot was lying on its side at the foot of red velvet drapes hung in front of a low Moorish-style arch.

The inspector went into the carpeted room, looked around, came back to the "waiting room", and back to the foyer which was actually nothing but a roofed passage that led from the building out into the street.

It was very hot in the second room. A smell of mint mixed with thyme floated in the air. One of the two Arabs, the one who seemed to be the owner, kept going from room to room, busy doing nothing.

The inspector came back into the "waiting room", examined the rubble, jotted something into a notebook, picked up a scrap of iron, put it in his pocket.

It was stifling. A grilled window opened onto a small courtyard. If one leaned forward a little, one could see the sky and stars through palm fronds. One could clearly hear the sound of the waves. After all, the shore was very close. The house must have been built right up against the city wall.

The entire section was steeped in silence. The sky was clear and wide...It was easy to climb over the city wall, cross the ocean drive, continue on the dirt road...

The inspector said: "That's only a warning. The first time..." Then he said goodbye and left. The curious bystanders must have gone back inside. One might as well leave.

It was at least a quarter to three. A fresher breeze blew in through the little window, carrying a scent of algae and salt. The palms swayed softly. One ought to be able to see the ocean from the terrace, the shorefront on the left and the port on the right, the ships, the jetty and, straight across the pebble point skirted by the ocean drive --a finger of naked land, four or five hundred yards long, with the ruins of the old lighthouse at its tip (the dirt path that leads up to it follows the ocean drive not far from Bab-el-Bahr, very close to the tin-can town that has lately sprung up in the elbow of the shore, circles the tin-can town, passes behind the skeleton of a fishing boat that lies on its flank not far from the rocks, straddles the middle of the point, runs through the ruins of two white houses, turns toward the open sea, goes almost up to the old lighthouse, runs in front of the brick villa with the shed surrounded by tamarisks...).

One might as well leave...Suddenly, soundlessly, the velvet curtain was pulled aside by a small hand, with a clinking of sliding bracelets; three quarters of a young girl's face appeared for a split second above the curtain, time enough to notice a delicate rose tatoo between the eyebrows, a black curl falling on a cheek, very dark eyes, teeth glittering in the half-light and, far behind, at the other end of a candle-lighted room, four other extremely young girls sitting on cushions, clad in yellow and lavender *serouals,* looking toward the door, nudging each other with their elbows, holding back giggles, for a split second, until the curtain dropped back.

The "owner" came up, rubbing his hands with clasped fingers. He smiled, repeated: "It's nothing"..."It's not so bad".

In the foyer, his colleague had just about finished sweeping up the rubble. The policemen were waiting in the street, ready to climb back into their jeep. Two of them stayed behind to stand guard outside the door.

The street was empty, the sky clear, the air cool.

The little Fiat had no trouble turning around in the alley, it didn't take long to get back to the ramparts. The policemen followed. They stopped at Bab-el-Bahr, immediately after passing the gate.

The ocean drive was completely deserted. Some hundred yards to the left stood the bandy-legged silhouette of the tower that marks the outpost of the old city nearest the ocean. On the right, the paved road followed the foot of the walls and disappeared at the first bend. On the other side of the road stood the rows of mud huts and corrugated metal shacks of the Haitian section, a kind of small shanty town that has sprung up in the elbow of the shore in recent years, at the base of the pebble point. A dog, startled by the headlights or by the noise, jumped up on the embankment and began barking in the direction of the car, then ran after it up to where the dirt road branches off, that no sign marks, which one can only guess by the gradual sloping of the sidewalk over two to three yeards, down to the road level.

The dog stopped there, climbed back up on the embankment, its head still turned toward the car.

Three o'clock, possibly a little later. It was a good time to return to yesterday's spot, to do a little investigating on the spur of the moment, to go and see what went on down there at night. Since the night had been interrupted at any rate, sleep irretrievably lost...

The car slowed down and turned left into the dirt road, the dog started to bark again, then ran along on the other side of the embankment, along the thorny hedge that borders the shanty town and through which appear, at each arbitrary turn of the wheel required by the holes in the road, here a wooden shack, there a hut of coarsely joined metal sheets, tin walls covered with tar, torn wire mesh, iron rods, barbed wire, and everywhere kettles, barrels, piles of bottles and tin cans, rusty stoves, pane-less window frames, bent pipes, bits of mirror which the sea wind was jiggling like shooting targets at a carnival. Each hole was a puddle; at the point where the road runs very close to the rocks the lighthouse beam struck a blanket of fog that masked the waves, then swept over the hull of the abandoned fishing boat; after that the road turned right, away from the shore, toward the ruins of houses.

The dog had stopped barking. It had not gone beyond the shanty town. Rails ran along the left of the road, the vestiges of a narrow-gauge railroad that probably supplied the old lighthouse. Tails of fog hung here and there across the way. The houses couldn't be far off. At any rate, fog or no fog, it was more prudent to stop the car behind a stretch of wall and continue on foot.

Sixty feet ahead, a white wall showed it's profile on the right in the lighthouse beam. Since there was no ditch, the operation posed no problem, the car stood well protected behind the house, with the headlights switched off.

The air was very cool. The sound of the waves covered the steps --the sound of shoes kicking a stone, crunching on pebbles. Gusts of wind made the shirt stick to the damp skin. Again and again blades of white brightness passed overhead, high up in the sky, swung in from the other side of the port, lost themselves in the open sea, far beyond the coast, skimmed at top speed over the invisible waves.

The night was black, the sky extremely pure, the fog rarer on this side of the point. It was less than two hundred yards from the broken-down houses to the brick villa, two hundred yards of straight walking between low walls of dry stones and jujube hedges behind which one could easily duck if need be. Abruptly the thorny hedge changed to tamarisk bushes: there stood the villa at the far end of the enclosure, with the shed on the left, a little farther back.

No light inside the villa, no light in the shed. A few yards beyond the gate the tamarisk hedge stopped, or rather, it continued at a right angle to the road, in the direction of the shed, closed by a sliding door. The sign out front could not be seen. An oblong shape, covered with a tarpaulin, stood between the leaves and the wall of the shed, it could be a canoe or a motor boat, a car more likely, or a small truck --yes; definitely a car; on the porch of the villa an electric bulb had just lighted up and illuminated the enclosure. A man appeared in the doorway, chewing on a pipe, came down the steps, walked into the enclosure. The tarpaulin was either too short or not completely unfolded --it was sucked in at the windshield-- leaving the front of the car uncovered: the large headlights at the tips of the fenders, the radiator grill looking like a giant set of false teeth and, just above, the oval shield of the make appeared clearly through the branches. The man walked as far as the gate, relit his pipe, then turned, retraced his steps, climbed back up on the porch, closed the door.

Darkness returned.

The night felt blacker now, the villa even more silent, more asleep.

On the way back, the fog blanket stretched almost without interruption --the fog horn had begun to groan-- if it had not been for the bend in the road, near the white houses, they would have been invisible.

The car was soaking wet. The humidity had come in through the open windows and dampened the imitation leather seats.

The yapping of the dog announced that the shanty town wasn't far off: but the boat had disappeared, and so had the tracks, the rocks, the tin walls, the barbed wire. From the lights along the ocean drive fell a diffused brightness of a very pale, diluted yellow. Visibility was five to six yards at most. Nevertheless, a strident whistle blew at the approach to Bab-el-Bahr; two policemen came up, cradling submachine guns; when they recognized the car, they saluted and walked away.

A police patrol at the Trois-Palmiers intersection ordered another halt. Then nothing between that and arrival at avenue du Port.

It was ten to four.

Sunday, four a.m.

At seven, the alarm went off. The big black car was there, down below, on the avenue --the big chrome grill, the oval shield with the name of the make in italics on a red background-- recognizable at once by the gaping hole in place of the windshield. An hour later it started its motor, trailed the Fiat as far as Spanish Square, satisfied with its brief ride --a very brief reminder that it was there-- whereupon it turned off, lost itself in the business district, disappeared for the rest of the day.

All was quiet at the Office. The Commandant was still in the same mood as the day before: jumpy, groping for words, unable to find them, he made a clumsy attempt to pick up the discussion, quickly dropped it of his own accord, afraid that he might say something unfortunate if he got excited, something that might shift the argument in a direction opposed to his intentions.

There was little news to comment on, except for last night's incident about which nobody had anything interesting to say. Answering the mail, putting the files in order, reading the memos that had accumulated during the week, took up the major part of the morning, as it did every Sunday. Everything would have been taken care of by noon if there had not been the announcement, about a quarter past eleven, that shots had just been fired near the covered market.

Going there was inevitable. The policemen had already arrived. The victim, a public scribe, lay stretched across the street, with two tiny holes in the back of his neck. The bullets had not come out in front, they formed two small conic protuberances under the forehead, which readily disappeared under the pressure of a finger, then rose up again. Inspector Lacoste arrived a few minutes later, with a worried expression ("Our last informer", he blurted out at one point.). As usual there were a dozen or so jeeps and various other vehicles parked at close range, and some twenty members of the military and civil service standing about, contemplating the spectacle from different distances, varying according to their ranks, all obliged, for different reasons, to be present at the scene of

the drama, all inquiring, taking notes, measuring, photograph-
ing, questioning, conjecturing, investigating.

Finally, after a long wait, the ambulance arrived and took
the body away. An old man came out of a house with a broom,
a large rag and a bucket of water.

It was noon, or ten after. The only thing to do was go to
lunch, then back to Avenue du Port to take a nap and make up
somewhat for the fatigue of the week.

At the time of waking, at four o'clock, the avenue was pretty
empty: people go to the beaches, desert the city, don't return
before nightfall when it's cooler.

But at five o'clock, exactly at the same time as the day before, the big Buick came slowly rolling down the avenue from
Roosevelt Square; it parked along the curb some thirty yards
from the entrance of the building.

Perez remained behind the wheel. As on the previous day,
Marietti began to polish the radiator grill, the headlights, the
bumper, the rims of the wheels --he does it either to kill time,
or it's a mania: quite visibly the car itself has not been washed
in weeks-- walked two or three times around the car, opened
the front door and slipped into the seat. At that point, or soon
after, Perez climbed out, paced a while under the trees, crossed
the avenue, had to wait a few seconds for the traffic that had
begun to stream back into the city, stepped up on the opposite
curb and sat down on the bench. It was six o'clock --no, five
thirty at most. The clock had just finished striking six when
Marietti took the wheel...It must have been five after six then,
ten after, maybe...He drove off in the direction of the port, but
he can't have gone very far, maybe not even beyond the gates
of the park. (But today he was still there long after six. Perhaps he had not moved at all, or else he had left long ago and
Perez had stayed on the bench. Or he had left with Perez. Or
else...)

He reappeared soon after, parked the car along the opposite

curb, almost in front of the bench on which Perez was half stretched out, smoking cigarettes. He sat down beside Perez (perhaps he is sitting beside Perez this very minute). They bought the paper, read it, smoked cigarettes; they chatted a bit...

They chatted...

They chatted, smoked cigarettes, read the paper.

At seven o'clock, or just before seven, or shortly after seven...

PART III

A brief, surprisingly clear tinkling echoes up the stairwell, followed by a cascade of clicks, as though a handful of marbles or nickels had been thrown full force on the tile floor, scattering, bouncing from step to step.

Then all grows quiet again.

Not another sound from beyond the door... Somebody must have dropped his keys, or his change, at the foot of the stairs. And he is picking everything up, or else he has already gone... Perhaps he was going downstairs, on his way out...If not, he can't have climbed up very far; certainly not beyond the fourth floor: or else one would hear his footsteps, distant, light and hollow thuds that one hears so easily, several floors away, within this completely enclosed sound-space, on the carpetless, echoing steps...

Not the faintest sound is coming up...There is still time to go out onto the landing and take a look, just in case, to ward off surprises.

The knob clicks, the lock tongue slides back, the door of the room pivots slowly on its hinges. Through the slit appear the top of the stairs, then the banister spindles, and, a little farther over to the left, behind the banister, the grillwork cage rising from the depths of the building, rising a few yards more up to the roof terrace which it seems to pierce with its metal rods.

The elevator is no longer there.

The landing is deserted...

From the elevator door one can see the entire floor below, then, at an angle, the major part of the flight between the sixth and fifth floors, a smaller portion of the flight between the fifth and fourth floors...Further down the grillwork hides all the other parts of the staircase that should, theoretically, be visible. The landings lie, of course, out of sight. The elevator itself has probably remained on the ground floor.

There is a sound of slow, regular steps, interrupted by throat clearing --soles rubbing across the imitation marble. The banister vibrates slightly.

The sound increases, grows more precise. Stops...The man must have reached the fifth-floor landing. He is taking a rest... The banister vibrates again, immediately the thudding starts, clearer, louder, a sleeve comes into view, a hand running along the railing, a pot-belly, a grey jacket, the wide-rimmed straw hat of the next-door neighbor returning from work, forcing himself --for the exercise, he claims-- to climb the seven flights each evening.

His breath comes in gasps. His body seems heavier with every step. Now he turns, climbing toward the sixth floor...

He has almost reached the sixth floor. He coughs. Squares his shoulders.

Raises his head toward the seventh-floor landing...

The movement was not unexpected. Besides, the wide rim of the hat delayed its effect. Immediately, silent feet tiptoe away on the dusty floor of the landing.

The door pivots, closes soundlessly. The fat man has not had the time to notice anything, and since the window is closed, he cannot have heard any noise from the avenue that might have made him suspect that the door of the room was open.

The door knob clicks, but very softly. The bolt slides home in two movements.

The distant, muffled, closed-out sounds from the avenue complete with the panting rhythm of foot falls that keep growing louder outside the door, mixed with the shocks traveling along the banister railing, the rustling of a piece of paper being unfolded, the sound of keys jingling on the chain. The footfalls become a shuffling of shoes, a short dry coughing spell, the scraping of a key groping for the keyhole. The door opens... The keys jingle once more, then the door slams, negligently pushed shut. More coughing, but less loud, the steps recede... The neighbor has gone straight into the kitchen.

It is at least seven o'clock, even a few minutes after seven. On the table, the stationery is still in the same position, unchanged, the top sheet still blank, or almost blank, the letter unfinished --not even begun; only the date has been written down at the top on the left: *Monday, August thirteen*...The letter will have to be started all over again this evening, if possible; or at the latest tomorrow at the office --during fifteen free minutes in the late morning; or else set the alarm a little earlier, get there ahead of time and write it quickly before the work starts pouring in.

The light is less raw than it was a while ago, but still strong; it seems to ooze out of the walls, the ceiling, the curtains, as though from a nearly autonomous source. It slides over the night table drawer, the chair arms, the red patterns in the rug, the grey cotton bed spread, hits the shelves at an angle, the gold-stamped volumes, the ochre-varnished perfume burner; it stumbles against the chair legs, the feet of the table, the wardrobe doors, the bakelite telephone, the alarm clock case... Only the white stone chandelier resists; its unchanging dull finish preserves it from all glossiness, from all transitory luster.

The straight-falling, motionless curtains cover the full width of the bay window. Far behind shimmer broken lines, vague shapes, tarnished colors veiled in gold and grey at the limits of sky and ocean.

The window handle turns, pivots, utters a long creak...A brusque gesture pulls the frames back, slowly they detach themselves one from the other, uncovering countless scattered buildings, gardens, avenues, hills, ships, twenty miles of shore-line, and beyond an enormous moving blanket ringed by a hardly perceptible border that is partly hidden by a deep pow-dery red that stretches from one end of the horizon to the other.

The sun is setting...

The sun is slipping behind a screen of black-grey-purple clouds piled into pyramids that seem to have accumulated in this particular portion of the sky solely to hide the brilliance of the declining rays to the last moment.

The air is much cooler. A light breeze makes the shirt stick to the damp skin. The delicate green, pale brown eucalyptus tops undulate along the entire perimeter of the park; in the center the bluish yellow palms sway gently, protected by the tall trees that surround them, lazily, like a lawn sown with giant grass. Beyond the park, on the terraces of the old city, a thou-sand pieces of cloth flap in the wind.

The lines have thinned, the surfaces have grown more pre-cise. They stand out more. Long shadows underline the masses, indicating everywhere the exact height of the eleva-tions that project them: on the terraces where they appear graded, on the metal scaffolding, the docks of the port, the jetty, the warehouse roofs, on the hills of the southern suburb where ample lavender crescents stand out in relief.

The ocean looks more distant, clearer, closer to the coast. The surface of the water has grown darker: it is neither blue nor green, more of a dark grey furrowed by opaque streaks that, in places, wear light foam caps snatched from the crests of the waves.

Many ships are in sight. One can see their complex, irregu-lar pitching easily when the hull shows itself in profile, not so easily bow on, although the almost imperceptible weaving of a mast, or a smoke stack is usually enough, even from a great distance, to show that the sea is extremely rough. An ocean liner is moving out to sea; its silhouette stands dark against the red sunset backdrop. Three large freighters are heading north, one behind the other, at equal distance, as though traveling in a convoy. An oil tanker is coming up from the south toward the harbor; it looks as though it were very close to the shore. But it may still be ten, fifteen miles off; the thought of its being still so far out endows it with enormous dimensions, for a moment, with inconceivable speed...No, it is really quite close to the shore, traveling at reduced speed, soon it will dock. Farther to the right, a fleet of fishing boats has just passed the jetty and is sailing toward the open sea: black, orange, blue sails swell, belly toward the surface of the water.

But the sky is rapidly changing. The clouds on the horizon fringe into a halo of fiery streaks, which seem to become more radiant, at first, as though the sequence from morning to night had been reversed, but this impression vanishes almost immediately as the halo begins to decrease; it sinks, shrinks perceptibly, breaks up into a multitude of purple dots that shine for another moment through the misty opacity, soon grow fainter, fade away.

The clouds over the land have scattered, drifted northward. The sky is a very pale blue, almost colorless, mainly clear. Another rainless day...

It has not rained for almost three weeks. The leaves are withering, the grass is turning yellow, the flowers hang their heads...The sprinkler goes on spinning at the other end of the lawn: the drops rain on the grass, on the long poinsettia stems, on the geraniums around the locker rooms, on the branches of the creeper that is climbing all the way up to the roof. The Arab boy is squatting on the steps of the restaurant, following the player's movements, their gesticulations. All the alleys are occupied, the games seem to progress very calmly, because it is much less hot, probably, and the quarrels tend to settle themselves automatically toward the end of the day. But anisette will revive them: the bar is constantly crowded; the clinking of bottles and glasses rings out clearly, very distinct from the neat, sharp sound of the balls clicking against each other.

The children are now playing on this side of the lawn, throwing a large ball that hits the brick wall several times; twice it almost goes over the top, almost on the sidewalk.

Surely somebody would pick it up and throw it back to them, before it rolled into the street among the cars. Many pedestrians pass on their way to the center of the city.

The Buick is parked along the curb, slightly to the left of the bench.

Perez and Marietti are sitting side by side on the bench, shoulder to shoulder, their heads close together, hunched over the evening paper which Perez is holding wide open with both hands. They have probably just bought it and are rapidly scanning the headlines, since Marietti already raises his head, draws back a little, sits up straight again, braced against the back of the bench, while Perez folds the paper into quarters, leans back and starts reading it methodically.

Perez is a good head taller than his buddy, but one can't tell that now. The two heads seem on the same level, so do the shoulders, Perez' bony and bent over, Marietti's broad, fleshy, muscled. One is half bald, the other has thick black heavily cream-oiled hair; one has prominent cheek bones, a long aquiline nose and greying temples, the other a low, unwrinkled forehead, a flattened nose and full rosy cheeks. Perez' long frame is molded by a white cotton sweater; his khaki trousers have been rolled up at the bottom, showing red socks and the straps of his leather sandals. All these days Marietti has been wearing a black and red wide-checked shirt with short sleeves that show his hairy arms, sunglasses, grey linen trousers and soft, probably old suede shoes. Occasionally he also wears a beige jacket, in the morning, for instance, but he must have left it in the car. Their revolvers are probably in one of the trouser pockets, either in the back pocket, especially made for that purpose, or more likely --for greater discretion-- in the right side pocket, since both are right-handers, one only has to watch the way they handle their keys, combs, rags, to see that they are.

Their looks, clothes, shapes, their gait --calm and ponderous in Perez' case; lively, bouncy in Marietti's-- everything about them is opposite, contradictory, even, except the persistent casualness both affect during the hours of watching (but that is borrowed behavior), except, of course, for the revolver which is, however, invisible, no one can tell that it's there.

It was quite different in the photograph. The contrasts were toned down: Marietti's forehead disappeared almost completely under the visor of his cap, so did Perez'; their skulls and hair were concealed. The noses remained (but head on the differences stand out less sharply), the cheeks (perhaps Marietti was thinner then? At any rate the contrast was not striking), the mouths...Nose, mouth, eyes (impossible to say, no recollection of their eyes) offered no independent interest, no individual characteristics, had been treated (by the subjects themselves, by their subordinates, their superiors, by the camera) as essentially plastic features, as mere accessories to their uniforms, a flesh substance that had been completely molded, fashioned by their function. Their identical attire --stiff leather visor, navy-blue cloth cap, the insignia of their squad, rigid collar, epaulettes, stripes-- all neutralized the contrasts, annulled the few still noticeable facial particularities.

United in the photograph, side by side, shoulder to shoulder on the front page of the evening paper (probably two old photographs pasted together), the two buddies displayed a frank, cordial smile just under the infamous headline ("Two policemen who fleeced Moslem stores in Saadia section"), a smile that seemed to express great self-satisfaction and pride, not only at the thought of having had their prowess publicized, but also with their recent arrest. Because they had been caught red-handed, had been arrested mercilessly: a brief introduction to the two-column report under the photo stated it bluntly.

The report itself was vaguer, more discreet; the curious reader learned at most that the double arrest had put an end to several months of reprehensible operation. But the papers didn't mention the matter the next day or the day after that. A week later, a brief notice appeared on the last page of the same evening paper, announcing that the inquiry into this "unfortunate affair" was taking its course, but everybody had already lost interest. All that was left was a bold-lettered headline at the bottom of the front page of a notorious scandal sheet, a photo-montage showing two practically interchangeable faces side by side, two easily-remembered names --two names, two easily-confused, interchangeable faces...

Names, headline, the exact position of the article (at the bottom on the right, on two columns), and the few details it disclosed all came back in a flash, two days ago, shortly after the first appearance of the two men behind the wheel of the old car, about one o'clock, on the winding roads of Aïn Zurka --and later, not much later, the date of the reported events: the end of last November, beginning of last December.

The memory revealed itself somewhat deficient as to which name went with which face. Besides, the point is secondary: whether the face on the left was Perez and the other Marietti, or vice versa, in no way affects the essentials of the matter. The long nose did seem to belong to Perez. The tall skinny guy, the lanky one with the thin white arms and large knotty hands was certainly Perez --and Marietti the short, stocky, sturdy one with the red face, the powerful muscles and erratic gestures.

Both placidly smiled from the front page of the paper, serene, sure of themselves, certain all the while that they were in no danger whatsoever. And rightly so, since nothing serious seems to have happened to them. They can't have been sentenced to anything, merely a routine disciplinary measure, a transfer to another division, a shift to a distant section. Or else they were dismissed without trial and in that case they are now continuing their job in a civil --a private-- capacity. It's not easy to find out, and actually it makes little difference: isn't the villa used by a mixed organization anyway?

An isolated villa on a deserted road next to a windowless shed, very close to the shore, rocks behind the tamarisk enclosure, the eddying splashing water, the pretext of an innocuous trade, invented or abandoned long ago...

A dirt road out on the old lighthouse point far away from the ocean drive, from all traffic, a dead-end road full of pot holes and puddles...

I thought it would be a good idea to go there right away. The old man's information was surely correct, since it concerned his son. If his son had been taken out there the evening before, there was still a good chance of finding him in the same place, provided one acted fast. On the other hand, the situation had all kinds of general inplications that far exceeded this specific case; looked at from that angle it was, perhaps, harmful to act too quickly...In the end, the various arguments annulled each other, were replaced by a new motivation: curiosity.

Old Lamrani took his leave. Slowly he crossed the courtyard, leaning on his stick, his green slippers scraped across the ground under his *djellaba*. Close to the gate he stopped, rummaged through his satchel, put his black glasses back on. Then he turned right and walked away: one could follow his white beard bobbing up and down against the dark red background of the houses on the other side of the street.

It was nine o'clock, ten after nine, Saturday morning. The Fiat had stayed in the courtyard, near the entrance steps. Saïd slipped into the front seat, folded his long legs, shoulders rounded, as usual, his forearms on his knees, hands dangling, his khaki skull cap squashed flat against the roof at each bounce of the car on the cobblestones in the alley. Trucks, wagons, hand-drawn cars were blocking the ocean drive. Better take the outer boulevards.

It was hardly more than a fifteen-minute drive. The old man had been sure of the location. His other son had watched all day, hidden near the white houses behind the embankment.

It was stifling hot. The shadows of the palms were drawing large irregular triangles on the asphalt of Boulevard de Suez. A moderate breeze blew along the water front. Spray stolen from the crests of the waves splashed against the windows.

-You know the dirt road around the Haitian *derb* that leads out to the old lighthouse? You know?

The old man spoke a monosyllabic, repetitive, quavering Arabic...

After the Moorish tower on the left-hand side of the road come rows of mud and plank huts, shacks of tarred canvas, metal plating, corrugated tin; jujube bushes grow through the barbed wire on the flat embankment. The embankment decreases a little farther ahead, the curb stones disappear gradually over a two to three yard stretch, marking the beginning of the dirt road.

-He saw. He hid near the white houses, before the bend. He waited the whole day...

The road runs around the shanty town, passes in front of a small creek, very close to the rocks. Then comes the right turn, just before the beached boat, a straight stretch parallel to the narrow-gauge railroad tracks, then the white houses, the left turn, another stretch straight ahead, between low dry-stone walls, with the abandoned lighthouse at the end, and, on the right, the tamarisk enclosure, the shed, the villa.

The road was bumpy. Saïd's head knocked against the roof. A dog ran along the thorny hedge in front of the car, barking constantly. One could see women and children moving about among the *Gourbis,* lugging buckets, earthen jugs, kettles, bundles of wood. A child sat on a sand pile, scratching his scalp with his nails, another child, astride a barrel, was rubbing his fly-covered eyes. Garbage was heaped up in the middle of the alleys, dogs lay stretched out on their sides, men squatted in the shade; some turned their heads at the sound of the motor. A tall man in a black *gandoura* was hammering nails into a plank. Everywhere small slivers of mirror reflected the light, throwing brief flashes that reverberated from alley to alley, from tin wall to tin wall, in all directions, endlessly. Through the gaps between rows of shacks one could see the bending shoreline at the other end of the *derb,* and the whitish foam that covered the busy surface of the water.

Old Lamrani is sitting at the window, both hands on his stick which rises straight between his knees, his white beard concealed in the sleeves of his *djellaba.* His hoarse exhausted voice sometimes rings very clear at the end of a sentence, recites in a broken-up monotone, punctuated by questions.

-The police came. They took many people this week, you know. During the night...The police came to my house. Thursday evening. During the night...

Then comes the blue hull of the beached fishing boat, lying on its side, covered with brown streaks. Saïd knows the road well, he has relatives who live in the shanty town. One passes between the two broken-down houses, turns left, drives straight ahead on the last stretch, flanked by low dry stone walls and jujube hedges, to the abandoned lighthouse. Saïd said nothing, although he didn't know the destination. Perhaps he did know...

-They came for him. My son Brahim...

Afterwards they took him to the police station. Friday morning he was still there. The old man is certain. He knows someone at the station, an Arab guard, who told him for sure. Afterwards...

The little car bounced along the road. Its springs squeaked. It was tilting far to one side, with its right wheels up on the grass.

Large-lettered inscriptions in black paint covered the walls of the nearest houses: a patriotic slogan, the initials of a dis-

banded movement, a half-erased exclamation of revenge...
Saïd didn't open his mouth during the entire ride. He was
looking straight ahead. Perhaps he knew also.

Then came the bend. The car turned left, one wheel on the
grass, the other on the hump in the middle of the road. The
tamarisk hedge came into view and behind it the flat roof of
the villa.

-He watched the whole day. Yesterday.

-How?

-He hid. Near the houses...

-But how did he know?...

The old man sits motionless, leaning forward, both hands on
his cane. He has taken his dark glasses off. His grey motionless eyes are cast down...

-We know. It's been going on for about a month. Things
get around fast among us. We know...

Large low clouds came drifting in from the open sea, but
the point still lay in the sun. The shadow of the tamarisk drew
an uneven fringe on the sand which was now replacing the
chalky lumps and angular pebbles in the stretch of road behind.

Beyond, one could see the old wall, a few white terraces
looking out over the old city and further up in the sky: a pale
strip, gilt-edged on its southern end, a pink dust floating in the
air.

The sky is a very pale blue, almost colorless, completely clear. The clouds have scattered, fled toward the north, dragged along by the wind from the open sea. Far off the coast, a ring of mist masks the line of the horizon, a grey mist, the color of tarnished silver toward the bottom and lighter toward the top, fringed with yellow at the spot where the sun has disappeared.

The two shadow zones in the room, on either side of the bay window, have grown wider. Two wavy lines run along the rug, follow the track imprinted by the coming and going of feet; broken lines zig-zag across the table, the blotter, the blank top page of the letter pad, across the armchair whose own shadow is now stretching as far as the foot of the bed, a split diagonal.

The air is cooler.

Down on the ocean, the blue, orange and black sails of the fishing fleet lie almost flat against the waves.

The freighters are much farther out, toward the northwest. Only two are visible now --unless the first two have fused into one at this distance.

The tanker has stopped at the entrance to the port. It barely moves.

The ocean liner has disappeared.

Marietti stands up. He walks around the bench, two or three yards along the curb, bends down, picks something out of the gutter --the ball the children have finally thrown over the wall. He walks to the foot of the wall, throws the ball with his right arm, the way one might lift a weight, the arm raised above the shoulder. He wipes his fingers on his handkerchief, walks back to the bench. The children on the lawn continue the game which has been interrupted for an instant.

Perez quickly lowers his head. He had been looking up into the air. He must have noticed that the window was open. He leans toward his colleague, whispers something brief. Marietti, already reaching for his paper, shrugs, sinks back comfortably, becomes engrossed in the front page.

The *Bocce* players are engaged in an animated discussion, their arms make incomplete circular gestures that are lost in the leaves behind them, against the dark background of trees in the park. The light is fading.

It is twenty after seven on the clock over the locker rooms.

In the bar, the lights have already been turned on.

Down on the bench, the two silhouettes sit side by side, squashed by the plunging perspective, motionless.

It was in an identical pose, side by side in the car, that they appeared for the first time, on Saturday, early in the afternoon, not quite four hours after the scene at the villa.

I was leaving the *Restaurant de la Plage* on the Aïn Zurka promenade. The Fiat was parked in the shade of the palms that overlook the beach. At that point nothing seemed unusual. Still, the Buick must have been right there, either inside the restaurant lot, or not far on the promenade, its occupants stationed on a stone bench facing the ocean, or lounging against the parapet, keeping an eye on comings and goings, ready to start their motor in a hurry, as they must have done an hour before, outside the Office, otherwise they would never have gotten the idea of coming out here, so far from the center, to hunt down their prey. Perhaps they had stayed too far behind to make their presence known from the start, although that ought to have been their prime objective. But it isn't always easy to draw attention to oneself, even by the most evident maneuvers. It is perfectly possible that the image of their car may have appeared in the rear-view mirror for a fraction of a second at any given point or moment during the ten-mile ride from the old city out to Aïn Zurka promenade. But afterwards, at what point exactly did the presence of the car begin to make itself felt, trailing the Fiat on the winding boulevard back to the city?...At the first turn, perhaps, or shortly after?...At any rate, for sure at a point half-way down the coast road:

A bus was blocking a curve, forcing the cars behind it to slow down abruptly. At that instant, the front of a large black car that had kept up its previous speed appeared in the rear-view mirror, immediately monopolizing the entire oval surface that was playing back the reflections dancing on the hood, the radiator grill, the fenders, the headlights --as well as an absence of reflection in the windshield frame, mirroring a dark gap instead, with two silhouettes sitting inside, blurred at first, then abruptly, violently illuminated by the sun at the end of the curve-- two heads side by side, two dissimilar faces, but with the same air of familiarity as on the photograph.

The sound of an explosion; another, and a third, less loud --two echoes, or the last two thirds of a single explosion, chopped up by violent gusts of wind.

No, there were really three explosions --or just one, with its echoes in the head, or some ordinary racket amplified out of proportion...The ear seems to reproduce the three successive sounds endlessly, with decreasing intensity.

Down at the club, the players' motions freeze; they look up at the sky, ask each other questions, point their arms in different, opposing directions.

A pedestrian on the other sidewalk stops, walks on, nose skyward as though he expected a wall to crumble or a cloud of smoke to rise somewhere.

Cars, bicycles, carts, a bus move up and down the avenue as though nothing had happened.

Perez and Marietti are exchanging opinions. Marietti speaks with his nose in the paper. Then says no more. Perez looks right and left, lights a cigarette.

The noise must have come from the north, not from the old city: not a trace of smoke over the terraces. It that's not the case, the phone will start ringing any minute.

It sounded like a bomb somewhere near the *Quai aux Minerais,* or farther out still, in the industrial sections. Three bombs, to be exact. Explosions in an ammunition depot. Three bombs in the arsenal.

No smoke cloud, Anywhere. No trace of a fire. Not any-where along the entire visible stretch, from the port all the way to the hilly southern suburb. From the jetty to the bluish waves of the hills near Aïn Zurka.

The boulevard doesn't follow a strict course. Halfway down the slope, it splits into two roads which, in turn, split and wind, some shorter, some longer, around the hills at different heights, meet occasionally, split off again, all running together again halfway down the opposite slope around a flower-studded traffic circle, from which point the reunited boulevard takes a straight, four-lane-wide plunge toward the center of the old city.

I wanted to see --not to get away from them; just see if they'd follow.

The first road on the right started zig-zagging down the hill, between rows of villas, through wide, not too well banked curves, spindle-shrub hedges, mimosas and big shady trees, sumptuous houses, nestling in greenery, a rapid succession of well-ordered images, some across the full width of the wind-shield --the asphalt road unraveling at top speed, gravel side-walks, low walls, traffic signs rising up to meet the hood--, others higher up, in the little mirror above the windshield, as though on a small-scale movie screen --the same objects, fleeing at top speed in the opposite direction, growing smaller, flatter, running over each other, sliding, disappearing to the left, to the right, escaping the tiny frame--, two uneven strips of asphalt cut back into each other on the screen of the wind-shield, bend, twist, then a hundred and eighty degree turn starts up toward the top of the hill, in ten yards it makes up for the lost difference in altitude, fifty yards, a hundred yards, two hundred yards, the same greyish strip reflected, shrunken, in the oval mirror, with the last turn growing smaller and smaller at the end, yet perfectly visible, no other image is interposing itself, nothing on the road ahead, nothing behind; the road starts to wind, several narrow curves, then another straight stretch of lovely houses with green tile roofs, bushes, creepers, through gaps in the ivy and wild vine one sees fountains surrounded by lawns, rectangles of limpid water glittering in the sunshine, bay windows with wrought-iron grillwork, geraniums lining porches, glimpses of gardens, palms, parasol pines, flaming iris, rose bushes around swimming pools, tennis courts, and all the way down, the hazy ocean, cars of different colors in driveways, under bowers, along curbs, on sidewalks, and suddenly the boulevard at right angles to the road, one of the main trunks of the boulevard with its two white lines on the asphalt; still nothing in back, the boulevard climbs gently, gets close to the top, another turn, a large curve, two cars in front rolling at a steady speed, after the curve a straight stretch --the reflection of the American car in the rear-view mirror, still halfway around the curve, a Buick, at least five years old, with rust stains on the hood, windshield removed, a dent in one fender, the man beside the driver half asleep on the seat, hands behind his neck; he sits up straight, puts on dark glasses, leans against the door.

The boulevard was sloping downhill...

Still no sign of anything unusual over the old city. A fire could have started a little while after the explosions, the smoke appearing only now...But there isn't any smoke... Nothing.

And the telephone isn't ringing.

The boulevard sloped downhill, branched off, sloped gently. On the right lay the plain, the rocky fields, stones, the pink hazy plain, apparently with no contours whatever, completely flat.

I stepped on the accelerator, passed the two cars in front,

quickly turned left into a deserted lane.

A pebbly lane that climbed, winding through pines, palms, cypresses, turned once, turned twice, stopped in front of an impressive gate flanked by Venetian metal lanterns.

Only one alternative: to turn around, drive back out on the boulevard. At the side of the lane a sign warned: "Private road".

They were parked along the curb, a hundred yards from the turn-off, placidly waiting. The dark stocky one who had sat on the right was strolling under the eucalyptus trees, gazing up at the tops, his arms behind his back.

The traffic circle wasn't far off, and from then on the wide boulevard with its speed limit and red lights. Obviously they had started up again and were following, but relatively far behind.

Only back in the center of the city did they pull closer. Were they going to follow all the way to the Office?

A good method for getting rid of them was to enter the old city by an alley that was too narrow for them to squeeze through. Bab el Quedim was ideal for that kind of maneuver: the Buick could go in, but hadn't the slightest chance of getting through the turns of the next alley.

They didn't even try to go in. Before Bab el Quedim they slowed down, then continued directly along the foot of the old walls: the image of the Buick slipped out of the rear-view mirror at the very same instant the bumper of the Fiat grazed a stone marker at the corner and started to jiggle and clatter like a fiesta rattle, rattling down rue Sidi-Fettach, rattling constantly, like a piece of junk, all the way into the courtyard of the Office.

The Commandant was already at his desk, red-faced, with sweat-glistening forehead and brusque gestures, even more nervous than usual.

As usual, the shutters were closed, had been closed since early morning for fear of the heat, but the brightness that filtered through the wooden slats is more than adequate to light the room --the large, file-stacked table, the lamp, the telephone, the three visitors' armchairs, the plain chairs along the walls, the metal coat locker, the map of the old city tacked to the wall behind the table; nevertheless, the electric lamp stays on all day, as though to remind everyone that entered that this was not a place of rest.

The Commandant was still at work, he had not gone home for lunch, he hadn't had the time; shortly before one, Inspector Lacoste had come to see him, also very nervous and worried, claiming that he hadn't known anything about it, that he was hearing about it for the first time, that he would never have authorized his subordinates to use a private house no matter what their reasons which, however, certainly weren't lacking, since they had been working in closer and closer quarters at the station, whereas down there, don't you see, the remoteness of the villa, the quiet, the calm, the good results of the operation...Still, from there to accepting the cooperation of a private organization, certainly not, there were regulations, after all, discipline, strictly respected limits. No, this was going too far.

-I told him, I found this was going too far. Not that I wasn't aware of their difficulties, actually I can't blame them. The conditions they work under...the limited space...And as to the methods, that's their business. Everyone his own. And if it's the only way...But this working hand in hand with an underground group is going too far. Between you and me, I'm no patsy, he obviously has a hand in it. Either it's his idea, or he closed his eyes. The proof is that no one was surprised by

what you said when you arrived. I repeated it to him, natur-
ally...

The inspector had shrugged. What did that prove? Only
that the others, having been surprised, had let themselves be
impressed, no more. He added that he hadn't much appreci-
ated this appearing on the scene, this cavalier way of getting
into the act.

-I must admit that I, too...Please understand, as things stand
we have nothing to gain from making enemies of...

His hand trots back and forth across the table, nervously,
crawls over the files, wavers, hunches, flattens.

Already in the morning after the return from the villa, under
the eternally lighted lamp, those brief, erratic movements had
agitated the fingers, the hand hurried from file to file, seized
the handkerchief, the glasses, the same tics jerked across the
purplish face.

-It's most embarrassing, you understand...It should have
been done some other way, with more flexibility. Whereas
now...

Now, he explains, it will be much harder to settle the matter:
so many minor details, so many little quirks to humor...And
be especially careful that nothing of this leaks out.

-If only you had informed me, instead of going there at once,
and by yourself...He and I would have gone out there together.

As for nothing leaking out...Lamrani knew everything long
ago. His whole family knew, the whole Arab city.

The "Arab telephone" would make sure everything was
known, silently. Saïd would see to it, if necessary, perhaps
he had already done so. Silently, at night.

Saïd's fingers were around the handle, he was leaning against
the door, all ready to get out.

The door of the villa opened. Two men appeared on the threshold, at the top of the steps, even before the Fiat slowed down to pass the hedge.

I stopped the car exactly at the gate, facing the stoop. Saïd opened his door first, got out, opened the gate, stepped aside.

A wooden fence doubled by a row of bushes runs around the enclosure. It is covered by a layer of unevenly distributed gravel, furrowed by tire tracks. The shed stands on the left, a little farther back than the villa; it is built of concrete blocks and corrugated tin, and can also be used as a garage, but its sliding door was closed. A black Citroën was parked in front of the shed. Over the door hangs a wooden sign with grey, half faded letters, reading:

A. FERRERO

Plumbing — Metal Work

Bathroom Installations

Three steps --protected by a glass awning that supports an electric lamp in a cone-shaped enamelled metal shade-- lead up to the door of the villa. The ground floor has two windows, so has the second floor, and there is a small bull's eye above the awning.

All the shutters are closed, except those of the window to the right of the steps. The bull's eye has no shutter: its pane is divided into four even portions by cross bars. The brick work that shows through across the entire façade gives the building an unfinished look. The roof terrace slopes down toward the back...

The old man described the villa, his eyes half closed; his voice hoarse, panting, reciting, as though he knew the place well. At times one hears only the sucked-in breath and the gargling consonants of chopped-up syllables. And yet, words emerge from this foggy landscape of sound, their meaning can be guessed after a moment or two.

-You'll see. There is a garage on the left. A garage, or a workshop...On the front of the garage there is a sign. The name is Ferreira, Ferrari, something like that...But they don't work there any more, they haven't for a long time...

He didn't mention that the courtyard behind the building, or the door at the back of the villa, or the other door at the back of the shed, or the second gate in the middle of the rear fence, exactly symmetric to the one facing the steps.

The gate opens onto a sandy strip, overgrown with juniper, tufts of jujube and castor-oil plants, some fifty yards from the rocks, algae, and yellowish foam wobble in the water holes.

The place is completely deserted, the villa close to the shore, well protected from prying eyes.

-I think I know the place, says the Commandant. I drove to the lighthouse once, a year ago. I remember the road perfectly...I thought the buildings had been abandoned.

If it weren't for the cars parked inside the enclosure, they would still look abandoned: bolted shutters, chipping whitewash, rusty metal fittings, loose tin plates, badly trimmed hedges, with branches growing in all directions...

The sign on the wall of the shed, a board that was once painted white, the paint peeling off, rotting, with streaks of rust and oil, the letters half gone: plumbing, metal work...

The pretext of an innocuous trade, the cover of a fictitious profession, or else a genuine one, long since abandoned...

Saïd had stepped aside, holding the gate open with his left arm. Some ten yards to walk from the gate to the stoop, some fifteen steps to reach them...

There I was, walking on the gravel, with Saïd close behind me, practically at my side. The two men over there weren't moving. The car didn't mean anything to them, probably, no more than its driver (unless one of them had recognized both right away from a visit to the Office, one day, when he had seen them in the courtyard; but that was rather unlikely); it was probably Saïd's uniform that intrigued them, that discouraged immediate action or violent abuse.

They just stood and waited, in silence; they were standing in shadow, one could not tell them apart. The only sound was the crunching of the gravel underfoot and perhaps also the far-away sound of the surf against the rocks, muffled by the obstacle of the buildings.

In the silence that accompanied the walk across this ridiculous distance the legs seemed to move in place and not advance, the feet stepped up and down rhythmically, as though they were on a rolling carpet that ran in the opposite direction, the walls slid past smoothly, like a well-oiled theatre set, the two silhouettes were slowly, irresistibly, drawing closer, motionless and blurred, side by side on the top step, suddenly they were there, very close, at arm's length.

-You'll see, they are six or seven down there. Two policemen from the station, you probably know them, I don't know their names, and then the others, civilians, my son says the fat dark-haired one owns a cafe at the Palmeraie and the tall blond one runs a garage not far from the port, the others he doesn't know, ex-policemen maybe, or former soldiers, perhaps he does know, he didn't say.

Old Lamrani shells out his words in a quavering voice. He came very early, waited a long time outside the office door, leaning against the wall with hanging arms, head bent back, like a blind man.

His information turned out to be correct. Every detail as he had said.

-So there is Guillaume, from the old city station, as well as Latour. About the others we're hardly any further...

The Commandant goes over it once more, sums it up, scribbles on a piece of paper.

-And the car? Ah, you have the license number...

He jots down the number of the car, leafs through the telephone book, takes the receiver off the hook.

The telephone didn't ring.

It's a good fifteen minutes since the explosion. It wasn't in the old city then. But in the industrial sections, or farther north.

Marietti is still reading. Perez looks completely asleep.

Three short explosions, brutally shattering the silence...

-I've come to see Brahim Lamrani. Inspector Lacoste told me I'd find him here.

The tone is right, the voice clear and self-assured. Now the steps must be climbed at once, without hesitation.

At the second step the two men pull back, mechanically step aside. One of them says: "Inspector Lacoste", but there is no question in his voice, not even a doubt, he simply repeats the name to establish the notion in his head.

One of them (the other one, probably) says: "Go call Ruiz", and he points with his thumb to the door to the left of the foyer.

We are four in the foyer of the villa, a kind of fairly wide corridor. Through a half-open door on the right one can look into a room furnished with a table, a couch and two armchairs. Magazines lie spread out on the table, as in a dentist's waiting room. At the end of the corridor, a hot plate, a tank of butane, a sink.

Contrary to expectations the two guards differ as little from one another as they did before, while they stood in the shadow on the stoop: same height, same coloring, same expression --short and swarthy, pale, tired looking, crumpled white shirt with sleeves rolled up, extremely hairy arms.

Saïd is leaning against the door that has been closed again. The momentarily open door on the left reveals a bare room that is very dark because of the closed shutters; wooden boxes are stacked against the wall that joins the shed.

The man who went in to get Ruiz is now seen from the back, at the opposite end of the room walking toward a small door that faced the first one.

This is the moment Saïd chooses to walk down the corridor, hands behind his back, and go calmly into the dark room, on the heels of the man in the frame of the other door who is speaking to someone who must be sitting because, although he is quite short, he is bowing his head, and he is speaking in such a low voice that one cannot clearly hear him from the corridor.

The villa, then, has an inside connection with the shed (iron door, small wooden staircase). The shed itself may be forty-five by twelve or fifteen feet. It has a cement floor. The light enters through head-high windows in the wall parallel to the villa. On a bench all kinds of tools...

The report to the Commandant mentions only the essentials, an extremely sober description of the place and the people. In turn, the Commandant prunes, chops, reshuffles, puts the questions in order: time of arrival, location of the villa, layout of the shed, occupants.

There are eight men besides the two afore-mentioned guards --five standing up, three lying on the cement floor.

Two of the five are easy to identify: Latour and Guillaume,

two policemen from the old city station. They are not in uniform, but in civilian clothes: linen trousers and sports shirts. The others are not from the police: a tall, strong, powerful man with very dark cream-oiled hair flattened over his skull, a certain Ruiz, and two subordinates --definitely subordinates-- almost as stout as he, one blond with a scar across his right cheek, the other dark with a bashed-in nose.

The second group...

Several times the Commandant gets excited, stumbles over a sentence, repeats it, completely at a loss, as though all the meaning had gone out of it, he jumps when he hears a perfectly ordinary word that sounds strange to him, or misplaced, for the first time. But his tone remains courteous, moderate, halfway between persuasion and surprise.

To listen to him, the case is far from simple. Accomplices? That's easy to say. And who, he asks, will gain from a denunciation of abuses? ...His fountain pen carefully retraces the loops of letters, underlines a word, adds three dots here and there. The electric lamp spreads its drab, vague, superfluous light over the papers...In the end: the enemy, that's who, he concludes, no one else. Without taking into consideration, he affirms once more, that the police will never do anything against them especially not in this case. Try higher up? It would only multiply the obstacles, make trouble all around. "But don't think that I don't share your point of view, to a certain degree. Conniving with this gang, I must say..." The pen is doodling semi-circles, a triangle, something resembling a star. "...absolutely going too far. But from there to provoke a scandal, consciously, to slam doors behind one..."

The light that is coming in through the two windows is quite enough. A cement floor. A set of tools on a bench, iron boxes near the door to the back yard, barrels in a corner, a rubber hose attached to a spigot near the steps, a wooden tub in the center of the shed, three quarters full. There are puddles all over the cement, a small stream is flowing slowly from the tub to the door that opens onto the enclosure.

The gang comes from all walks of life: a barkeeper, former boxers, policemen (of indefinite age, low-echelon auxiliaries or recently dismissed civil servants), two still active policemen...A sole link unites them: the same desire to humiliate, to prove to themselves, at all cost, that they're still strong, although they know perfectly well that their movement has been ruled out and that its dissolution is imminent, but they hope to delay the deadline as long as possible, gain a couple of months, a couple of years, and until then --before it's all over-- go on hogging the middle of the road with impunity.

An odd gang: "The sons of A. Ferrero", with their cars, their helpers...Their accomplices in the Office, their handymen, who are given small daily chores, vigilant, needy, partly reassured at present: they're certain that the Commandant isn't going to take any measures, which makes them feel strong enough to wipe out the last obstacles; according to them, it is merely a question of patience and tenacity.

Their normal hour of departure has come. They should be leaving now. The car is parked nearby, along the curb. Marietti is still reading, or doing a crossword puzzle. Perez is dragging on his cigarette with an absent look. The *Bocce* players are continuing their games under the light of the lamps that hang from the branches.

Fewer cars pass on the avenue. Leaves are falling, autumn-like, on the pavement.

The second group consists of three Arabs.

The first Arab cowers in the corner of the wall, to the left of the steps beside the sliding door that opens out on the enclosure. His undershirt is covered with dark stains. Strands of damp hair fall over his forehead, stick to his skin. The right arm hangs lifeless down his body. His left hand is trying to lift a half-smoked cigarette to his lips, but the fingers are trembling and the lips won't open. His eyes are cast down; slight, helpless, regular tremors quake his chest and throat.

Saïd walks across the dark room and slowly, resolutely, toward the door to the shed. The guard draws back, steps aside. The other guard in the corridor doesn't budge, doesn't say a word...

The second Arab is on his knees in front of the tub. His head is leaning against the wooden rim. A rope ties his wrists behind his back. Water runs from his hair, drops on his shirt, his trousers, onto the cement floor of the shed, begins to form a small puddle in front of his knees. His mouth hangs open, his breath comes in gasps, panting, irregular. His eyes stare in the direction of the door which frames the two motionless men.

Saïd has stopped at the top of the steps, moved aside, left the passage free.

The fat man by the name of Ruiz is standing at the foot of the steps, his hands on his hips. He motions to the shed with his head, to all the people inside, raises his eyebrows, says with a wide cordial smile, without the slightest embarrassment: "You can see, we're helping each other out", or "Got to help each other out". (More precisely: "Got to lend each other a hand".) His two body guards, or subordinates, are standing in back of him --even here. Officer Latour, instantly recognizable, is sitting on a stool beside the tub, sleeves rolled up. Guillaume is standing at the other end of the shed, a coat over his shoulders; he is combing his hair, apparently on the point of leaving.

The third Arab is lying on the floor, under the bench, his face hidden, turned to the wall, his arms folded across his chest.

Lights are going on here and there, all around, have gone on, small pale glimmers in the direction of the sea, dulled by the vast over-all silver that glimmers ghostlike along the horizon, shiny dots that dance in the harbor and the southern sections against the dark background of the sky.

Distant lamp posts along the straight roads, the boulevards, the paths in the park. Groups of people are taking peaceful after-dinner strolls.

A calm day, almost uneventful...

Saïd said: Lamrani's son is over there, the one on the left, in the corner.

-What about that one down there?"

Guillaume pointed to the bench with his thumb, without turning around: "That one?" He burst out laughing.

The tall guy with the bashed-in nose wiped his forehead with the back of his hand, said in a voice almost like a chant: "He fell into the water."

Ruiz just stands there, hands on hips, a motionless, smiling mass, working his tongue around his mouth, staring calmly ahead of him, in the direction of the door.

Raw, intense, blinding light floods the room. The glare is unbearable: the lids close, blood mounts to the head, beats hard in the temples. A blinding brightness, a vast glittering blanket inundates the room, hits the naked walls.

Saïd enters, pulls the door shut behind him, freezes against the wood, without a word, without the slightest movement of the head, then pivots on his heels, glides soundlessly outside, vanishes.

Lamrani is sitting with his back to the window, hands folded around his cane that rises straight up between his knees. The vast sleeves of his *djellaba* partly conceal his white beard. His quavering broken voice shells out words, a stream of words, difficult to understand. Later he takes off his dark glasses, uncovers his grey, steady, immobile eyes.

The shutters are closed, as always, but the brightness that filters through the wooden slats adequately lights the room. Nevertheless, the electric lamp stays lighted all day long; it spreads a drab, even, useless light over the table, the files, the papers.

The Commandant says: "As far as the prisoners are concerned --Brahim Lamrani and the other one, I forgot his name--, that's been taken care of."

He explains: "He went down there immediately, as he had promised me, he brought them back to the station."

Continues: "Obviously it's necessary to make sure from now on that such incidents do not recur...and to make sure right now that none of this leaks out."

Moralizes: "A certain amount of abuse will always be inevitable...It's by staying on one's job mainly that...Besides, it has to be recognized that, apart from a few regrettable incidents..."

-What about the third?

-The third..." The Commandant remains silent, raises both hands at equal height above the table, leans forward, pushes his chin slightly forward, raises his head slightly, ruffles his eyebrows; his lips are closed, his eyes cast down.

It is past ten o'clock. The Office courtyard is full of people. Outside, under the windows, people are waiting in line along the walls, as always. The corridor remains crowded: fused whispers, secrecies, the slurring of slippers and sandals on the tiles, filter continuously through the closed door.

The door opens suddenly. The Commandant walks in. Saïd rushes forward, closes the door, disappears.

The Commandant takes the chair that is closest to the desk. For a moment he keeps his eyes fixed on the map of the old city that is tacked on the opposite wall. His left hand drums on the edge of the table. His eyes glide over the files, the papers, wander from object to object, rapidly, continuously, for a few brief seconds --a few seconds delay, a few last seconds of pondering before he asks the question, before he hears the answer.

Tomorrow morning...

The scandal is spread over the front page of the newspaper, two right-hand columns at the bottom of the evening daily's front page. Side by side, on the photograph, shoulder to shoulder, the two delinquents smile a frank, hearty smile, looking like brothers in the dark uniforms, under the caps that conceal their foreheads. Two old photographs, actually, maliciously stripped together, but the montage is well done, the picture is centered exactly over the headline, the un-informed reader might rightfully think that the two guilty partners were happy to pose for the camera, proud of their accomplishments.

It is only a minor scandal, the kind one allows to get into print. Their crimes aren't terribly serious. Obviously the two buddies didn't smile the evening of their arrest, but their faces express neither shame nor embarrassment, not even any fear of tomorrow, hardly even surprise.

Confidence returns, signs of group spirit, of solidarity make themselves felt. They will soon be released, transferred to another division, to another district, or perhaps they will even be relieved of their duties. But they don't care, they won't be out of a job for long.

A gang recruits them, tries them out, soon after that they're entrusted with minor outside missions, observation, shadowing, driving through the city, the business district, the suburbs, the outskirts, minor daily chores that soon become routine, boring.

Their early-morning eagerness slackens well before noon, as soon as they're half through the day, their energy evaporates, attention strays, the sieges grow longer, hour upon hour, smooth, monotonous, indifferent.

Always the same streets, the same familiar buildings, the same rounds through the city, the same open stretches of road; the day passes mechanically, just as it does at the office, in the patient expectation of going home.

Perez is still sitting in the same place, hands flat on the bench at either side of his thighs, his head resting against his left shoulder; he was probably tired and has finally dozed off. Marietti seems to be through with his paper, or else he just stopped, also because he was tired, perhaps; the paper lies spread out before him, half on the bench and half on his knees, as though it had fallen out of his hands.

The shadows under the leaves expand, pile up. It is growing very dark around the bench. The sidewalk, the street seem to have receded, the cobblestones, the asphalt seem to have sunk a couple of yards, into the bottom of a deep, dusk-invaded ditch.

A car slips out of the parked line in front of the building, gains the middle of the road, drives off noisily. At the same instant, all the glass globes along the avenue light up, operated by an inaudible switch.

Perez lifts his head, rubs his eyes, looks at his watch, slaps his neighbor on the shoulder. Marietti starts, yawns, stretches luxuriously, catches the paper that was sliding into the gutter.

Beyond the sidewalk, the brick wall hardly stands out against the lawn behind it. The zone of darkness stretches all the way to the club buildings where most of the players are meeting for dinner. Through the wide bay window of the restaurant one can see men sitting around tables, talking. All the alleys are empty, except the last one on the right; where an undecided game is about to be finished. A fat man with a napkin around his neck is calling to the dawdlers from the door of the restaurant; several times he calls out to them; points to the clock.

The lamps in the trees make the grounds look like an abandoned fair. A song is heard from time to time, an easy melody with a two-beat rhythm.

The clock over the locker rooms, feebly lighted by a bulb outside the entrance, says five to eight.

Perez got up, walked to the car with heavy steps. He opens the door, slips behind the wheel, presses on the starter, steps hard on the accelerator, then lets the motor idle, puts the headlights on, taps the horn twice, calling his colleague to order, since he's still sitting on the bench.

Marietti signals that he is coming, sits up, readjusts his belt, looks up, casts a mechanical glance toward the top floors of the building, but he can't see much beyond the halo of yellow brightness projected by the street lamp, he probably just sees a naked plain housefront, the windows lost in the grey of the walls. He doesn't insist, he walks to the curb, up to the car, opens the door, slips into the front seat. The door slams.

Perez turns the wheel to extricate himself from the line of parked cars, starts, heads for the middle of the road, drives off at top speed in the direction of Roosevelt Square.

In a few seconds the old Buick had disappeared between the double row of leaves that line the avenue.

The room is plunged in semi-darkness, it's not actually very dark --the sky is still light enough to let one read at the window, without the lamp-- but the lamps along the avenue continue to dance before the eyes and objects barely stand out against the persistent intermittent glare that destroys their outlines. But by and by the important lines affirm themselves, as do the dark masses of the table, the bed, the shelves against the white wall, the smooth white stone chandelier with its dull finish, against the lavender-colored map of the old city.

The purring of the elevator comes clearly through the closed door, the sound of nasal voices --not a whisper, a firm voice, with a clear, regular intonation-- through the door and through the wall of the apartment next door: "Sunny tomorrow in all parts of the country, morning fog along the coast, temperatures higher than today".

The radio diffuses a constant breathy hissing, never accentuated but always perceptible, even when the window is open, punctuated by over-positive statements and irrepressible jingles.

Other sounds come through the wall: a clinking of forks, a glass against the mouth of a bottle, a chair leg scraping the tiles.

The curtains sway. A gust of fresh air sweeps all the way into the room, into the narrow aisle between table and bed, along the white wall where the lighthouse beam makes multi-shaped, oversized shadows file past during the night, shreds of shadows that spin like tops.

But now the lighthouse is nothing but a tiny bright glimmer, blinking at regular intervals --eight seconds, six seconds, three seconds-- at the very tip of the jetty, toward the north, not far from the spot where the tanker is anchored, parallel to the channel; the tanker must have its lights on, but they are invisible, or blocked by a building that stands in the way.

The fishing boats are gone; or else their lights are far too weak to be seen at this distance. The entire surface of the water looks smooth, monochromatic, the eye can only guess, can only slide over an open, even, intangible surface. For the first time this day, the line of the horizon stands out clearly --and for the last time, since, in a few seconds, sky and water will blend into total impenetrable darkness.

Numerous small erratic lights glitter on the hills of Aïn Zurka, headlights on the avenue, lamps in the villas, alternately veiled and unveiled by swaying branches.

A star shines in the south, dimly, very high up in the cloudless sky.

Closer, rows of lamp posts, looming above the trees, perfectly, although intermittently, retrace the continuous belt of the outer boulevards, a broken, uneven line bounding a vast semi-circle on the perimeter of the modern city.

Still closer, against a mixed back-drop of half shadows that blurs all evaluation of distance, rise the tall new buildings on the right, and the cathedral on the left.

The park is empty. The strollers have gone home. Others --or the same ones-- will come back after dinner. For the moment, the paths lie deserted, a pink brightness falls from the top of the branches onto the empty space between the wickets around the lawn, a diffused brightness, as though diluted with dust and spray. Four wrought-iron lamps around the central circle illuminate the statue whose imperial gesture and call to war seem no longer addressed to anyone in particular.

In the park, the palms barely move. Only the balding eucalyptus fronds around the edges continue to sway.

And beyond the park, between park and ocean, between the port and residential sections, stretches a large whitish patch, slightly wavy and hard to distinguish: the eye sees it only by looking at its edges --by focusing on the horizon, or on any given point along the shore, further north or further south. Not a single light shines on the thousands of terraces that compose it, not a single human being shows his face. Thousands of white houses standing wall to wall, as though built at random into the narrow available space, compressed between the winding, curving alleys into which nobody ventures any more, where only soldiers walk after nightfall, up and down all night long, index on the trigger, ears straining --every hour of the night, rhythmically, slowly, up and down the tiny streets, cats and dogs fleeing at their approach, only the hammering of boots on the pavement, weapons clinking, brief, worried commands, sudden explosions echoing through the labyrinth of dark little streets, quickly muffled in blind alleys where the sound dies against high windowless walls. The next morning, at the first ray of dawn, windows slam, doors open a slit, people slip out of their houses, the dock workers walk with rapid steps, hurry toward the port, the streets come alive, the iron curtains go up, crowds gather, women step slowly forward, old men, young people pass huddled on trucks, sounds of a flute, of a strident nasal violin, filter out of the Moorish